LAST BREATH

Karin Slaughter is the #1 internationally-bestselling author of more than a dozen novels, including the Will Trent and Grant County series and the instant *New York Times* bestsellers *Cop Town* and *Pretty Girls*. There are more than thirty-five million copies of her books in print around the world. She lives in Atlanta, Georgia.

For more information visit Karinslaughter.com
Facebook.com/AuthorKarinSlaughter
@SlaughterKarin

Also by Karin Slaughter

Karin Slaughter

LAST BREATH

HarperCollins*Publishers*

HarperCollins*Publishers* Ltd
1 London Bridge Street,
London SE1 9GF

www.harpercollins.co.uk

This paperback edition 2017

First published in Great Britain in ebook format
by HarperCollins*Publishers* 2017

A catalogue record for this book
is available from the British Library

ISBN: 978-0-00-826062-0

Set in Sabon by Palimpsest Book Production Limited, Falkirk, Stirlingshire

Printed and bound in the UK

MIX
Paper from
responsible sources
FSC **FSC C007454**
www.fsc.org

Find out more about HarperCollins and the environment at
www.harpercollins.co.uk/green

June 8, 2004

1

"Come on now, Miss Charlie." Dexter Black's voice was scratchy over the jailhouse payphone. He was fifteen years her senior, but the "miss" was meant to convey respect for their respective positions. "I told you I'm'a take care of your bill soon as you get me outta this mess."

Charlie Quinn rolled her eyes up so far in her head that she felt dizzy. She was standing outside a packed room of Girl Scouts at the YWCA. She should not have taken the call, but there were few worse things than being surrounded by a gaggle of teenage girls. "Dexter, you said the exact same thing the last time I got you out of trouble, and the minute you walked out of rehab, you spent all of your money on lottery tickets."

"I could'a won, and then I would'a paid you out half. Not just what I owe you, Miss Charlie. Half."

"That's very generous, but half of nothing is nothing." She waited for him to come up with another excuse, but all she heard was the distinct murmur of the North Georgia Men's Detention Center. Bars being rattled. Expletives

3

being shouted. Grown men crying. Guards telling them all to shut the hell up.

She said, "I'm not wasting my anytime cell-phone minutes on your silence."

"I got something," Dexter said. "Something gonna get me paid."

"I hope it's not anything you wouldn't want the police to find out about on a recorded phone conversation from jail." Charlie wiped sweat from her forehead. The hallway was like an oven. "Dexter, you owe me almost two thousand dollars. I can't be your lawyer for free. I've got a mortgage and school loans and I'd like to be able to eat at a nice restaurant occasionally without worrying my credit card will be declined."

"Miss Charlie," Dexter repeated. "I see what you were doing there, reminding me about the phone being recorded, but what I'm saying is that I got something might be worth some money to the police."

"You should get a good lawyer to represent you in the negotiations, because it's not going to be me."

"Wait, wait, don't hang up," Dexter pleaded. "I'm just remembering what you told me all them years ago when we first started. You remember that?"

Charlie's eye roll was not as pronounced this time. Dexter had been her first client when she'd set up shop straight out of law school.

He said, "You told me that you passed up them big jobs in the city 'cause you wanted to help people." He paused for effect. "Don't you still wanna help people, Miss Charlie?"

She mumbled a few curses that the phone monitors at the jail would appreciate. "Carter Grail," she said, offering him the name of another lawyer.

"That old drunk?" Dexter sounded picky for a man wearing an orange prison jumpsuit. "Miss Charlie, please can you—"

"Don't sign anything that you don't understand." Charlie flipped her phone closed and dropped it into her purse. A group of women in bike shorts walked past. The YWCA mid-morning crowd consisted of retirees and young mothers. She could hear a distant *thump-thump-thump* of heavy bass from an exercise class. The air smelled of chlorine from the indoor pool. *Thunks* from the tennis courts penetrated the double-paned windows.

Charlie leaned back against the wall. She replayed Dexter's call in her head. He was in jail again. For meth again. He was probably thinking he could snitch on a fellow meth head, or a dealer, and make the charges go away. If he didn't have a lawyer looking over the deal from the district attorney's office, he would be better off holding his nuts and buying more lottery tickets.

She felt bad about his situation, but not as bad as she felt about the prospect of being late on her car payment.

The door to the rec room opened. Belinda Foster looked panicked. She was twenty-eight, the same age as Charlie, but with a toddler at home, a baby on the way and a husband she talked about as if he was another burdensome child. Taking over Girl Scout career day had not been Belinda's stupidest mistake this summer, but it was in the top three.

"Charlie!" Belinda tugged at the trefoil scarf around her neck. "If you don't get back in here, I'm gonna throw myself off the roof."

"You'd only break your neck."

Belinda pulled open the door and waited.

Charlie nudged around her friend's very pregnant belly.

5

Nothing had changed in the rec room since her ringing cell phone had given her respite from the crowd. All of the oxygen was being sucked up by twenty fresh-faced, giggling Girl Scouts ranging from the ages of fifteen to eighteen. Charlie tried not to shudder at the sight of them. She had a tiny smidge over a decade on most of the girls, but there was something familiar about each and every one of them.

The math nerds. The future English majors. The cheerleaders. The Plastics. The goths. The dorks. The freaks. The geeks. They all flashed the same smiles at each other, the kind that edged up at the corners of their mouths because, at any time, one of them could pull a proverbial knife: a haircut might look stupid, the wrong color nail polish could be on fingernails, the wrong shoes, the wrong tights, the wrong word and suddenly you were on the outside looking in.

Charlie could still recall what it felt like to be stuck in the purgatory of the outside. There was nothing more torturous, more lonely, than being iced out by a gaggle of teenage girls.

"Cake?" Belinda offered her a paper-thin slice of sheet cake.

"Hm," was all Charlie could say. Her stomach felt queasy. She couldn't stop her gaze from traveling around the sparsely furnished rec room. The girls were all young, thin and beautiful in a way that Charlie did not appreciate when she was among them. Short miniskirts. Tight T-shirts and blouses opened one button too many. They seemed so frighteningly confident. They flicked back their long, fake blonde hair as they laughed. They narrowed expertly made-up eyes as they listened to stories. Sashes were askew. Vests were unbuttoned. Some of these girls were in serious violation of the Girl Scout dress code.

Charlie said, "I can't remember what we talked about when we were that age."

"That the Culpepper girls were a bunch of bitches."

Charlie winced at the name of her torturers. She took the plate from Belinda, but only to keep her hands occupied. "Why aren't any of them asking me questions?"

"We never asked questions," Belinda said, and Charlie felt instant regret that she had spurned all the career women who had spoken at her Girl Scout meetings. The speakers had all seemed so old. Charlie was not old. She still had her badge-filled sash in a closet somewhere at home. She was a kick-ass lawyer. She was married to an adorable guy. She was in the best shape of her life. These girls should think she was awesome. They should be inundating her with questions about how she got to be so cool instead of snickering in their little cliques, likely discussing how much pig's blood to put in a bucket over Charlie's head.

"I can't believe their make-up," Belinda said. "My mother almost scrubbed the eyes off my face when I tried to sneak out with mascara on."

Charlie's mother had been killed when she was thirteen, but she could recall many a lecture from Lenore, her father's secretary, about the dangerous message sent by too-tight Jordache jeans.

Not that Lenore had been able to stop her.

Belinda said, "I'm not going to raise Layla like that." She meant her three-year-old daughter, who had somehow turned out to be a thoughtful, angelic child despite her mother's lifelong love of beer pong, tequila shooters, and unemployed guys who rode motorcycles. "These girls, they're sweet, but they have no sense of shame. They think everything they do is okay. And don't even get me started

7

on the sex. The things they say in meetings." She snorted, leaving out the best part. "We were never like that."

Charlie had seen quite the opposite, especially when a Harley was involved. "I guess the point of feminism is that they have choices, not that they do exactly what we think they should do."

"Well, maybe, but we're still right and they're still wrong."

"Now you sound like a mother." Charlie used her fork to cut off a section of chocolate frosting from the cake. It landed like paste on her tongue. She handed the plate back to Belinda. "I was terrified of disappointing my mom."

Belinda finished the cake. "I was terrified of your mom, period."

Charlie smiled, then she put her hand to her stomach as the frosting roiled around like driftwood in a tsunami.

"You okay?" Belinda asked.

Charlie held up her hand. The sickness came over her so suddenly that she couldn't even ask where the bathroom was.

Belinda knew the look. "It's down the hall on the—"

Charlie bolted out of the room. She kept her hand tight to her mouth as she tried doors. A closet. Another closet.

A fresh-faced Girl Scout was coming out of the last door she tried.

"Oh," the teenager said, flinging up her hands, backing away.

Charlie ran into the closest stall and sloughed the contents of her stomach into the toilet. The force was so much that tears squeezed out of her eyes. She gripped the side of the bowl with both hands. She made grunting noises that she would be ashamed for any human being to hear.

But someone did hear.

8

"Ma'am?" the teenager asked, which somehow made everything worse, because Charlie was not old enough to be called ma'am. "Ma'am, are you okay?"

"Yes, thank you."

"Are you sure?"

"Yes, thank you. You can go away." Charlie bit her lip so that she wouldn't curse the helpful little creature like a dog. She searched for her purse. It was outside the stall. Her wallet had fallen out, her keys, a pack of gum, loose change. The strap dragged across the greasy-looking tile floor like a tail. She started to reach out for it, but gave up when her stomach clenched. All she could do was sit on the filthy bathroom floor, gather her hair up off her neck, and pray that her troubles would be confined to one end of her body.

"Ma'am?" the girl repeated.

Charlie desperately wanted to tell her to get the hell out, but couldn't risk opening her mouth. She waited, eyes closed, listening to the silence, begging her ears to pick out the sound of the door closing as the girl left.

Instead, the faucet was turned on. Water ran into the sink. Paper towels were pulled from the dispenser.

Charlie opened her eyes. She flushed the toilet. Why on earth was she so ill?

It couldn't be the cake. Charlie was lactose intolerant, but Belinda would never make anything from scratch. Canned frosting was 99 percent chemicals, usually not enough to send her over the edge. Was it the happy chicken from General Ho's she'd had for supper last night? The egg roll she'd sneaked out of the fridge before going to bed? The luncheon meat she'd scarfed down before her morning run? The breakfast burrito fiesta she'd gotten at Taco Bell on the way to the Y?

9

Jesus, she ate like a sixteen-year-old boy.

The faucet turned off.

Charlie should have at least opened the stall door, but a quick survey of the damage changed her mind. Her navy skirt was hiked up. Pantyhose ripped. There were splatters on her white silk blouse that would likely never come out. Worst of all, she had scuffed the toe of her new shoe, a navy high-heel Lenore had helped her pick out for court.

"Ma'am?" the teen said. She was holding a wet paper towel under the stall door.

"Thank you," Charlie managed. She pressed the cool towel to the back of her neck and closed her eyes again. Was this a stomach bug?

"Ma'am, I can get you something to drink," the girl offered.

Charlie almost threw up again at the thought of Belinda's cough-mediciney punch. If the girl was not going to leave, she might as well be put to use. "There's some change in my wallet. Do you mind getting a ginger ale from the machine?"

The girl knelt down on the floor. Charlie saw the familiar khaki-colored sash with badges sewn all over it. Customer Loyalty. Business Planning. Marketing. Financial Literacy. Top Seller. Apparently, she knew how to move some cookies.

Charlie said, "The bills are in the side."

The girl opened her wallet. Charlie's driver's license was in the clear plastic part. "I thought your last name was Quinn?"

"It is. At work. That's my married name."

"How long have you been married?"

"Four and a half years."

"My gran says it takes five years before you hate them."

10

Charlie could not imagine ever hating her husband. She also couldn't imagine keeping up her end of this under-stall conversation. The urge to puke again was tickling at the back of her throat.

"Your dad is Rusty Quinn," the girl said, which meant that she had been in town for more than ten minutes. Charlie's father had a reputation in Pikeville because of the clients he defended—convenience store robbers, drug dealers, murderers and assorted felons. How people in town viewed Rusty generally depended on whether or not they or a family member ever needed his services.

The girl said, "I heard he helps people."

"He does." Charlie did not like how the words echoed back to Dexter's reminder that she had turned down hundreds of thousands of dollars a year in the city so that she could work for people who really needed her. If there was one guiding ethos in Charlie's life, it was that she was not going to be like her father.

"I bet he's expensive." The girl asked, "Are you expensive? I mean, when you help people?"

Charlie put her hand to her mouth again. How could she ask this teenager to please get her some ginger ale without screaming at her?

"I enjoyed your speech," the girl said. "My mom was killed in a car accident when I was little."

Charlie waited for context, but there was none. The girl slid a dollar bill out of Charlie's wallet and finally, thankfully, left.

There was nothing to do in the ensuing silence but see if she could stand. Charlie had fortuitously ended up in the handicapped stall. She gripped the metal rails and shakily pulled herself up to standing. She spat into the toilet a few times before flushing it again. When she opened

11

the stall door, the mirror greeted her with a pale, sickly-looking woman in a $120 puke-spotted silk blouse. Her dark hair looked wild. Her lips had a bluish tint.

Charlie lifted her hair, holding it in a ponytail. She turned on the sink and slurped water into her mouth. She caught her reflection again as she leaned down to spit.

Her mother's eyes looked back at her. Her mother's arched eyebrow.

What's going on in that mind of yours, Charlie?

Charlie had heard this question at least three or four times a week back when her mother was alive. She would be sitting in the kitchen doing her homework, or on the floor of her room trying to do some kind of craft project, and her mother would sit opposite her and ask the same question that she always asked.

What is going on in your mind?

It was not contrived to be a conversation starter. Her mother was a scientist and a scholar. She had never been one for idle chitchat. She was genuinely curious about what thoughts filled her thirteen-year-old daughter's head.

Until Charlie had met her husband, no one else had ever expressed such genuine interest.

The door opened. The girl was back with a ginger ale. She was pretty, though not conventionally so. She did not seem to fit in with her perfectly coifed peers. Her dark hair was long and straight, pinned back with a silver clip on one side. She was young-looking, probably fifteen, but her face was absent make-up. Her crisp green Girl Scout T-shirt was tucked into her faded jeans, which Charlie felt was unfair because in her day they had been forced to wear scratchy white button-up shirts and khaki skirts with knee socks.

Charlie did not know which felt worse, that she had

thrown up or that she had just employed the phrase, "in her day."

"I'll put the change in your wallet," the girl offered.

"Thank you." Charlie drank some of the ginger ale while the girl neatly repacked the contents of her purse.

The girl said, "Those stains on your blouse will come out with a mixture of a tablespoon of ammonia, a quart of warm water and a half a teaspoon of detergent. You soak it in a bowl."

"Thank you again." Charlie wasn't sure she wanted to soak anything she owned in ammonia, but judging by the badges on the sash, the girl knew what she was talking about. "How long have you been in Girl Scouts?"

"I got my start as a Brownie. My mom signed me up. I thought it was lame, but you learn lots of things, like business skills."

"My mom signed me up, too." Charlie had never thought it was lame. She had loved all the projects and the camping trips and especially eating the cookies she had made her parents buy. "What's your name?"

"Flora Faulkner," she said. "My mom named me Florabama, because I was born on the state line, but I go by Flora."

Charlie smiled, but only because she knew that she was going to laugh about this later with her husband. "There are worse things that you could be called."

Flora looked down at her hands. "A lot of the girls are pretty good at thinking of mean things."

Clearly, this was some kind of opening, but Charlie was at a loss for words. She combed back through her knowledge of after-school specials. All she could remember was that movie of the week where Ted Danson is married to Glenn Close and she finds out that he's molesting their teenage daughter but she's been cold in bed so it's probably her fault so they all go to therapy and learn to live with it.

"Miss Quinn?" Flora put Charlie's purse on the counter. "Do you want me to get you some crackers?"

"No, I'm fine." Remarkably, Charlie *was* fine. Whatever had made her stomach upset had passed. "Why don't you give me a minute to clean myself up, then I'll join you back in the rec room?"

"Okay," Flora said, but she didn't leave.

"Is there anything else?"

"I was wondering—" She glanced at the mirror over the sink, then back down at the floor. There was something delicate about the girl that Charlie had not noticed before. When Flora looked up again, she was crying. "Can you help me? I mean, as a lawyer?"

Charlie was surprised by the request. The girl looked nothing like her usual juvenile offenders who'd been caught selling weed behind the school. Her mind flashed up all the nice, white-girl problems: pregnant, STD, kleptomaniac, bad score on the SATs. Rather than guess, Charlie asked, "What's going on?"

"I don't have a lot of money, at least not yet, but—"

"Don't worry about that part. Just tell me what you need."

"I want to be emancipated."

Charlie felt her mouth form into a circle of surprise.

"I'm fifteen, but I'll be sixteen next month, and I looked it up at the library. I know that's the legal age in Georgia to be emancipated."

"If you looked it up, then you know the criteria."

"I have to be married or in active service in the military or I have to petition the court to emancipate me."

14

She really had done her homework. "You live with your father?"

"My grandparents. My father's dead. He overdosed in prison."

Charlie nodded, because she knew that this happened more often than anyone wanted to admit. "Is there anyone else in your family who could take you in?"

"No, it's just the three of us left. I love Paw and Meemaw, but they're…" Flora shrugged, but the shrug was the important part.

Charlie asked, "Are they hurting you?"

"No, ma'am, never. They're…" Again, she shrugged. "I don't think they like me very much."

"A lot of kids your age feel that way."

"They're not strong people," she said. "Strong in character."

Charlie leaned back against the counter. She had left child molester off her list of possible teenage-girl problems. "Flora, emancipation is a very serious request. If you want me to help you, you're going to have to give me details."

"Have you ever helped a kid with this before?"

Charlie shook her head. "No, so if you don't feel comfortable—"

"It's okay," Flora said. "I was just curious. I don't think it happens a lot."

"That's for a reason," Charlie said. "Generally, the court is very hesitant to remove a child from a home. You have to provide justification, and if you really looked into the law, there are two other important criteria: you have to prove that you can support yourself without your parents, and you have to do this without receiving any aid from the state."

"I work shifts at the diner. And my friend Nancy's

parents said I could live with them until I'm out of school, and then when I go to college, I can live at the dorms."

The more Flora spoke, the more determined she sounded.

Charlie asked, "Have you ever been in trouble?"

"No, ma'am. Not ever. I've got a 4.0 GPA. I'm already taking AP classes. I'm on the Principal's Scholars list and I volunteer in the reading lab." Her face turned red from the bragging. She put her hands to her cheeks. "I'm sorry, but you asked."

"Don't be sorry. That's a lot to be proud of," Charlie told her. "Listen, if your friend's parents are willing to take you in, it might be that you can work out an arrangement without the courts getting involved."

"I've got money," Flora said. "I can pay you."

Charlie wasn't going to take money from a troubled fifteen-year-old. "It's not about money. It's about what's easier for you. And for your grandparents. If this goes to court—"

"I don't mean that kind of money," Flora said. "After my mama was killed in the car accident, the trucking company had to set up a trust to take care of me."

Charlie waited, but the girl didn't volunteer details. "What kind of trust?"

"It pays out for things like where I live and medical stuff, but most of it's being held until I'm ready to go to college, only I'm scared it's not going to be there when I'm ready to go."

"Why is that?"

"Because Paw and Meemaw are spending it."

"If the trust says they can only use the money for—"

"They bought a house, but then they sold it for the cash and rented an apartment, then they took me to the

16

doctor and he said I was sick, but I wasn't, and then they got a new car."

Charlie crossed her arms. "That's stealing from you and defrauding the trust. Those are both very serious crimes."

"I know. I looked that up, too." Flora stared down at her hands again. "I don't want to get Meemaw and Paw into trouble. I can't send them to jail. Not like that. I just want to be able to…" She sniffed. Tears rolled down her cheeks. "I just want to go to college. I want to be able to have choices. That's what my mama would've wanted. She never wanted me to get stuck where I didn't want to be."

Charlie let out a steady stream of breath. Her own mother had been the same way, always pushing Charlie to study harder, to do more, to use the gifts of her intelligence and drive to be useful in the world.

"She was good to me," Flora said. "My mama. She was kind, and she looked after me, and she was always in my corner, no matter what." Flora wiped her eyes with the back of her hand. "I'm sorry. I still miss her is all. I feel like I need to honor her memory, to make sure some good comes out of what happened to her."

It was Charlie's turn to look down at her hands. She felt a lump in her throat. She had thought more about her mother in the last five minutes than she had in the last month. The longing for her, the desire for one more chance to tell her mother what was on her mind, was an ache that would never go away.

Charlie had to clear her throat before she could ask Flora, "How long have you been thinking about emancipation?"

"Since after Paw's surgery," the girl said. "He hurt his leg three years ago falling off a ladder. He couldn't go back to work."

"He's addicted to pain medication?" Charlie guessed, because the Pikeville jail was filled with such men. "Be honest with me. Is it pills?"

The girl nodded with visible reluctance. "Don't tell anybody, please. I don't want him to go to prison."

"That won't happen because of me," Charlie promised. "But you need to understand that putting this in motion is a public thing. You won't be a protected minor anymore. Court records are out there for everybody to see. And that's not even the hard part. In order to prepare a petition supporting your request for emancipation, I'll have to talk to your grandparents, your teachers, your employer, your friend's parents. Everybody will know what you're doing."

"I'm not trying to do it on the sly. You can talk to anybody you want to, today even, right now. I don't want anybody to get into trouble, like go-to-jail trouble. I just want to get out so I can go to a good college and do something with my life."

Her earnestness was heartbreaking. "Your grandparents might put up a fight. You'll have to be blunt about why you want to leave. You don't have to mention the pills, but you'll have to tell a judge that you feel they're not good guardians for you, that you would rather be on your own than have to live with them." Charlie tried to paint a picture for her. "You'll all be in court at the same time. You'll have to tell a judge, in the open, in front of anybody who wants to hear, that you are unable to reconcile with them and you don't want them in your life in any capacity."

Flora seemed to equivocate. "What if they don't fight it? What if they agree with it?"

"That would certainly make things easier, but—"

"Paw has other problems."

Charlie's mind went straight back to the abuse issue. "Is he hurting you?"

Flora did not answer, but she didn't look away, either.

"Flora, if he's hurting you—"

The door opened. They both startled at the furious look on Belinda's face. "What are you two rascals doing hiding out in here?" She had tried to make her voice sound light, but there was no hiding her distress. "I've got a whole room full of girls back there with nothing to do but drink punch and talk about how dry my cake is."

Flora looked at Charlie. "It's not what you're thinking." There was a note of desperation in her voice. "I mean it. It's not that. Talk to whoever you need to. Please. I'll make a list for you. Okay?"

Before Charlie could answer, Flora left the bathroom.

"What was that about?" Belinda asked.

Charlie opened her mouth to explain, but she got stuck on Flora's desperate tone, her insistence that what Charlie was thinking was not what was actually happening. But what if it was? If the girl was being abused by her grandfather, that changed everything.

"Charlie?" Belinda asked. "What's up? Why are you hiding out in here?"

"I'm not hiding, I was—"

"Did you throw up?"

Charlie could only concentrate on one thing at a time. "Did you make that frosting from scratch?"

"Don't be stupid." Belinda squinted her eyes, as if Charlie was an abstract painting. "Your boobs look bigger."

"I thought your sorority taught you how to deal with those feelings."

"Shut up," Belinda said. "Are you pregnant?"

"Very funny." The only religious thing in Charlie's life

19

was the schedule by which she took her birth control pills. "I've been spotting for two days. I'm cramping. I want to eat candy and kill everything. I think it's just a bug."

"It better be a bug." Belinda rubbed her round belly. "Enjoy your freedom before everything changes."

"That sounds ominous."

"You'll see. Once you start having babies, that perfect, loving husband of yours will start treating you like a milk cow. Trust me. It's like they think they have something over you. And they do. You're trapped, and they know that you need them, but they can walk away at any time and find somebody younger and tighter to have fun with."

Charlie wasn't going to have this conversation again. The only thing that seemed to change about her friends with children is that they started treating their husbands like jerks. "Tell me about Flora."

"Who?" Belinda seemed to have forgotten the girl as soon as she left the room. "Oh, her. You know that movie we saw last month, *Mean Girls*? She'd be the Lindsay Lohan character."

"So, part of the group but not a leader, and not particularly comfortable with the meanness?"

"More like a survivor. Those bitches are next-level cruel." Belinda sniffed toward the handicap stall. "Did you eat bacon for breakfast?"

Charlie searched her purse for some mints. She found gum instead, but the thought of the peppermint flavor made her feel queasy again. "Do you have some candy?"

"I think I have some Jolly Ranchers." Belinda unzipped her purse. "Ugh, I should clean this out. Cheerios. How did those get in there? There's some mints. Oreos, but you can't—"

Charlie snatched the bag out of her hands.

"I thought you couldn't do milk?"

"Do you really think this white crap has milk in it?" Charlie bit into an Oreo. She felt an instant soothing in her brain. "What about her parents?"

"Whose parents?"

"B, keep up with me. I'm asking about Flora Faulkner."

"Oh, well, her mother died. Dad, too. His parents are raising her. She's a cookie-selling machine. I think she went to the ceremony in Atlanta last—"

"What are her grandparents like?"

"I've only been doing this for a minute, Charlie. I don't know much of anything about any of those girls except they seem to think it's easy to bake a sheet cake and throw a party for twenty snotty teenagers who don't appreciate anything you've done for them and think you're old and fat and stupid." She had tears in her eyes, but she had tears in her eyes a lot lately. "It's exactly like being home with Ryan. I thought it would be different having something to do, but they think I'm a failure, just like he does."

Charlie couldn't take another crying jag about Belinda's husband right now. "Do you think that Flora's grandparents are doing a good job?"

"You mean, raising her?" Belinda looked in the mirror, using her pinky finger to carefully wipe under her eyes. "I dunno. She's a good kid. She does well in school. She's an awesome Girl Scout. I think she's really smart. And sweet. And really thoughtful, like she helped me get the cake out of the car when I got here, while the rest of those lazy bitches stood around with their thumbs up their asses."

"Okay, that's Flora. What about her grandparents as human beings?"

"I don't like to say bad things about people."

Charlie laughed. So did Belinda. If she didn't say bad things about people, half her day would be spent in silence.

Belinda said, "I met the grandmother last month. She smelled like a whiskey barrel at eight o'clock in the morning. Driving a sapphire blue Porsche, though. A freaking Porsche. And they had that house on the lake, but now they're living in those cinder-block apartments down from Shady Ray's."

Charlie wondered where the Porsche had ended up. "What about the grandfather?"

"I dunno. Some of the girls were teasing her about him because he's good looking or something, but he's got to be, like, two thousand years old, so maybe they were just being bitches. You get teased about your dad all the time, right?"

Charlie hadn't been teased, she had been threatened, and her mother had been murdered, because her father made a living out of keeping bad men out of prison. "Anything else about the grandfather?"

"That's all I've got." Belinda was checking her make-up in the mirror again. Charlie didn't want to think in platitudes, like that her friend was glowing, but Belinda was a different person when she was pregnant. Her skin cleared up. There was always color in her cheeks. For all of her prickliness, she had stopped obsessing about the small things. Like she didn't seem to care that her watermelon-sized stomach was pressed against the counter, wicking water into her dress. Or that her navel poked out like the stem on an apple.

Charlie would look like that one day. She would grow her husband's child in her belly. She would be a mother— hopefully a mother like her own mother, who was interested in her kids, who pushed them to be intelligent, useful women.

22

One day.

Eventually.

They had talked about this before, Charlie and her husband. They would have a baby as soon as they had a handle on their student loans. As soon as her practice was steady. As soon as their cars were paid off. As soon as her nerdy husband was ready to give up the spare bedroom where he kept his mildly expensive Star Trek collection.

Charlie tried to do a running tally of how much the Emancipation of Florabama Faulkner would cost. Filing fees. Motions. Court appearances. Not to mention hours of Charlie's time. She could not in good conscience take funds from Flora's trust, no matter how much money was left in it.

If Dexter Black paid his bill, that might almost cover the expenses.

She heard her father's voice in her head—

And if frogs had wings, they wouldn't bump their tails hopping.

Belinda said, "Why are you asking all these questions?"

"Because I think Flora needs my help."

"Wait, is this like that John Grisham movie where the kid gives Susan Sarandon a dollar to be his lawyer?"

"No," Charlie said. "This is like that movie where the stupid lawyer goes bankrupt because she never gets paid."

2

Charlie kicked the vending machine in the basement of the courthouse. The glass rattled in the frame. She kicked it again. The bright yellow pack of Starburst shook on the metal spiral, but did not drop down.

Her shoe was already scuffed from puking in the bathroom. She raised her foot for another kick.

"That's government property."

She turned around. Ben Bernard, one of the lawyers from the district attorney's office, trundled down the stairs. The collar of his dress shirt was frayed. His tie was askew. He studied the stuck Starbursts. A large sticker on the glass warned that shaking the machine could result in fines and possible imprisonment.

He asked, "How badly do you want this?"

"Bad enough to go down on you in the supply closet if you get it for me."

Ben grabbed the machine with both arms and gave it a violent shake. Her husband was no Arnold Schwarzenegger, but he was clearly motivated. It only took two attempts. The Starburst dropped into the hopper. He reached down and pulled out the yellow pack with a flourish.

Charlie was game, but she warned, "I should probably confess that I had my head in a toilet twenty minutes ago."

"They put a lock on the door after the last time, anyway." He pressed his hand to her forehead. "You feeling okay?"

"I think it's PMS." She bit open the pack of candy. "Listen, I need to run a name past you."

Ben's mouth moved as he chewed at the tip of his tongue. They had been doing their respective jobs for four years, but he was a prosecutor and she was a defense attorney; they still hadn't quite worked out how to help each other while still maintaining their professional sides.

"It's not a criminal case," she assured him. "At least, not my part in it. I've got a girl who wants to be emancipated from her guardians."

He sucked air between his teeth.

"Yeah, it's not a great situation." Charlie tried to peel the wrapper off a red Starburst. "I was upstairs filling out a document request on a structured trust. The guardians are her grandparents. It sounds like they're into some bad things."

He took over for her on the candy wrapper. "What bad things?"

"Pills, I gather. And alcohol. And money from the trust. It sounds like they're going to milk it dry before she's of age."

"So, she can pay you?"

"Ehn." Charlie shrugged, giving what she hoped was a winning smile.

Ben said, "Dexter Black."

"Not my client."

25

"Yeah, I noticed that when Carter Grail brought him into the office for a talk. Any idea when he's going to pay you?"

"Babe, if my clients paid me, we'd probably end up taking a long vacation to somewhere like Costa Rica, and you would get really sunburned, which raises your risk for melanoma, which is the deadliest form of skin cancer, and then I would have to kill myself because I can't live without you."

"Okay, that makes a lot of sense."

Charlie could see that he was trying. "I'm not one hundred percent certain that she's not being abused."

"Shit."

"Well, she didn't tell me that she was being abused. She actually denied it, but..." Charlie shrugged again. She wasn't clairvoyant, but she'd had a bad feeling when she'd heard Flora's denial. There was a fleeting look in the girl's eyes, like she had been trapped in a corner and didn't know how to get out. "Even if it's not true, she's in trouble, and I feel like I have to at least try to help her."

Ben didn't hesitate. "Then, either way, I have to support your decision."

She had no idea how she'd managed to marry such a wonderful man. "We'll pay off our student loans one day."

"With our social security." Ben held up the candy. Charlie opened her mouth so he could drop it in.

He asked, "What's the girl's name?"

"Florabama Faulkner."

His eyebrows shot up. "Seriously?"

"Kid never had a chance." Charlie chewed the Starburst a few times before sticking it up inside her cheek. "Grandparents are raising her. She gave me their names, but I got their address from the Girl Scout rolls."

"That sounds vaguely illegal."

"I took a pledge to be a sister to every Scout, so it's basically like spying on my sister."

"I'm going to distract you with my hands while I try not to think about you wearing a Girl Scout uniform." Ben took out the tiny spiral notebook he always kept in his suit pocket. He showed the cover to Charlie: Captain Kirk looking serious about some Starship business. He edged the compact pen out of the spiral. He thumbed to a blank page.

She said, "Leroy and Maude Faulkner. They're living down from Shady Ray's."

His pen didn't move. "In the cinder-block apartments?"

"Yep."

"That's a bad place to raise a kid."

"They used to live on the lake. I'm assuming that trust fund mixed in with their addictions made it easy to make some bad decisions. Belinda says the grandmother showed up in a Porsche once, stone drunk."

"What kind of Porsche?" Ben shook his head. "Never mind. I get what you're saying."

"Flora wants to go to college. She wants to make her mom proud, to honor her memory. That probably won't happen if she stays with her grandparents."

"Probably not." Ben scribbled the names and closed his notebook. "Word around the office is the entire apartment building is under surveillance. The cops are being really secretive about it, but I saw some photos on the wall in Ken's office. Addicts live there along with a handful of terrified, law-abiding citizens who can't afford better. There's a meth lab in the vicinity."

"They can't find it?" Meth labs were usually found in trailers or recently blown-up basements.

Ben said, "I gleaned from the photos that they think whoever is cooking the meth is doing it out of the back of a panel van."

"That sounds stupid and dangerous."

"The cops will catch them the minute the van explodes." He tucked the notebook back in his pocket. "You sure you're okay?"

"Just thinking about my mom a lot. Flora's mother died when she was young. It stirred up some things."

"What can I do to make you feel better?"

"You're doing it." Charlie stroked her fingers through Ben's hair. "I always feel better when I'm with you."

They both smiled at the corny line, but they both knew that it was true.

He said, "Listen, I know I can't keep you away from those apartments, but don't go there alone, okay? Ask to meet them somewhere neutral, like for coffee at the diner. Whatever is going on at that place has to be dangerous. The county wouldn't be spending the money for surveillance otherwise."

"Understood." Charlie smoothed down his tie. She could feel his heart beating beneath her palm. She pressed her lips to his neck. The skin prickled to attention. She traced her mouth up, whispering in his ear, "I promise you'll get a rain check on the supply closet."

"Chuck," he whispered back, "this would be so hot if you didn't have puke in your hair."

Charlie swung by the house to take a shower and change before going to the cinder-block apartments. She had indicated to Ben an understanding that she should stay away from the place, but Ben probably knew that Charlie wouldn't stay away, so going there was actually living up to a long-held promise in their marriage: the promise that she would do whatever the hell she wanted.

She was happy to exchange her grown-up, career-day clothes for jeans and one of her Duke Blue Devils basketball T-shirts. Considering how much she and Ben owed the law school, she was surprised they hadn't been forced to wear sandwich boards until the loans were paid off.

The time was close enough to lunch for her to be hungry, so she ate a peanut butter and jelly sandwich and half a bag of Doritos while she dialed into the messages on her office phone. Charlie had a court appearance Friday and there was a last-minute motion to be filed. A judge was asking for a brief on a point of law that would not help her client. And because her life wasn't difficult enough, she had a call from her credit-card company that was likely not a warm thank you for being a valued customer.

Charlie searched the filing cabinet and found the previous month's bill, which, according to her handwritten note on the statement, had been paid a day late, but that didn't usually warrant a call. They were fifteen hundred dollars away from their limit.

Charlie called Visa on the number from the message. She was searching her wallet for her card when her cell phone rang. She kept her home phone to her ear while she answered the other one.

"Miss Charlie," Dexter said. "Please don't hang up."

"I think you meant to call Carter Grail."

"Come on, now, don't be like that. You told me to call the dude."

"Because you owe me two grand." Charlie listened to the Visa hold Muzak, a sax rendition of REM's "Losing My Religion".

Dexter said, "Lookit, Miss Charlie, I'm'a pay you Tuesday."

Charlie thought of Wimpy, who was always offering to pay people on Tuesday for a hamburger today, and then she realized that she was still hungry. "Dexter, I'll be really happy if you pay me, but I can't give you any legal advice until you do."

"But, lookit, it'll help you, too, 'cause like I said, I get paid, then you get paid."

"I'm not allowed to bargain with you like that. It gives me a vested interest in the outcome of your—shit." Her Visa card wasn't in its usual slot in her wallet.

"Miss Charlie?"

"I'm here." She rifled her wallet, her stomach in free fall until she found the Visa crammed between the dollar bills in the folded part.

The YWCA bathroom. Her purse spilled onto the floor.

Flora must have put the card back in the wrong place.

Dexter said, "I just need you to tell me can I do this thing I'm gonna do, and would I be okay if I didn't do the thing, like, exactly, because see, the person I'm dealing with, well, shit, let's just say they don't play."

"I can't negotiate for you in bad faith." Charlie saw the trap she'd walked into, because now she was giving him legal advice. "I'm not negotiating for you, period, Dexter. I can't tell you how to break the law. And if I was your lawyer, I couldn't put you on the stand knowing you were going to lie, and I couldn't allow you to sign a plea deal knowing that you intend to obfuscate."

"Obfuscate," he repeated. "Yeah, I know that word from *The X-Files*. Did you see that episode? Dude stuck this metal thing up people's noses and sucked the color outta their skin."

"Teliko," Charlie said, because her husband was a geek and they had every season of *The X-Files* in both VHS and DVD. "Dexter, is there something that I can help you with that won't involve me breaking the law, or advising you on how to break the law, or wasting the minutes on my cell-phone plan, or all three?"

"Uh…"

Charlie yawned. She suddenly felt exhausted. "Dexter?"

He waited a few more seconds, then asked, "What was the question again?"

Charlie hung up her cell phone.

Static filled the home phone at her other ear. The recording advised her that her hold time to speak with a Visa representative was only sixteen more minutes.

Charlie put the phone back on the hook.

She jammed the Visa bill into her purse for a later follow-up. She looked at the couch and thought about how nice a nap would be. And then she remembered Flora's situation. Charlie's calendar was generally full, but she had kept today light because she'd planned on an assortment of eager Girl Scouts wanting to ask her tons of questions about how to make their lives as awesome as Charlie's. If she was going to figure out how to help Florabama Faulkner, today was the only day she could do it.

She grabbed the Doritos on the way out the door and drove with the bag between her legs, carefully handling the chips, making a mental list of things she needed to do.

First, she would talk to Flora's grandparents and see if the situation was as bad as the girl claimed. The question of abuse was still unanswered. Maybe Flora had been honest in the bathroom and there was nothing untoward going on. Or maybe she was willing to sacrifice the truth in order to keep her grandfather out of jail. Or maybe Charlie had watched too many made-for-TV movies. Whether it was pills or neglect or abuse, the fact that Flora was actively working to keep her guardians out of jail said a lot about the girl's character.

Next on the list, she would need to get some idea of Nancy's living situation. That was the name of the girl whose parents had offered to take in Flora. Charlie had their address courtesy of the list Flora had made at the Y this morning.

The last thing on the list was to talk to Flora's boss at the diner to make sure the girl was gainfully employed. Or maybe it wasn't the very last thing. If there was extra time, she could make some calls from home to interview a few of Flora's teachers. Charlie had cut her teeth working juvenile cases. She knew that teachers saw a hell of a lot more than the average person in a child's life, even the parents.

That was a lot to fit into one day, but talking to people, sussing out the truth, was the hard part. The rest was just paperwork.

Charlie felt her stomach rumble. She felt sick, but she also felt hungry. She did the math again in her head, reminding herself that her period was due any minute now, that the spotting and the cramping and the soreness in her breasts and the PMS-induced hunger were all pointing to the same damn sign they pointed to every month.

She ate a handful of Dotiros as she passed an open semi-trailer filled with chickens. The chickens stared at her, but Charlie's thoughts were squarely on what Belinda had said about how being pregnant changed everything.

Charlie supposed that was the point, that things changed

when you had a baby, but from what she had noticed, it was like any big life event: either it brought you closer together or it pulled you apart. Ryan, Belinda's husband, had done a tour in Iraq as some kind of technical support person. So, he'd been in the desert, but not in the middle of combat. For a while, it seemed like he only came home to yell at the television set and make Belinda pregnant. War had changed him. Not just war, but the niggling suspicion that the war he was fighting was more like running in quicksand. The sense of futility was only part of the problem. The other part was the nature of his extended deployments. His long absences had given Belinda time to get used to making all of the decisions. When Ryan came back with different ideas about how things should be run, the tension had spilled over into every aspect of their marriage.

To Charlie's thinking, their main issue was usefulness. Both Belinda and Ryan wanted to have a purpose, to give their family direction, and both of them were making each other miserable because they couldn't share the responsibility.

Charlie laughed at her Oprah-esque observation. She had to blame her mother for this line of thinking. Charlie's childhood had been shaped by her mother's constant refrain—

If you're not being useful, then you're being useless.

Was Charlie being useful? Flora was so eager to carry out the life that her mother had envisioned. Charlie felt that same sense of urgency. Was she honoring her mother? Did her life have purpose?

It sure as hell lacked focus.

She'd been so zoned out that she had passed right by the cinder-block apartments.

"Shi-i-i-it," she drew out the word as she glanced behind her, catching the two-story building in her side-view mirror. She pulled a wagon wheel of a U-turn across the empty four-lane highway and pulled up at the two-story cinder-block building tucked down in a ravine behind a long stretch of busted guard rail. To her surprise, she saw that the apartments had a name. A discreet sign welcomed visitors to the Ponderosa. Ropes twined around the border in homage to the *Bonanza* TV show, but this was no place for Little Joe to hang his hat. Unless he wanted to crack open a light bulb and smoke a bowl.

The majority of the parking spaces were filled with beat-up old cars; not a good sign, considering most people should be at work this time of day. She drove to the end of the parking lot on the off-chance she would see the Porsche that Belinda had told her about, but Charlie's three-year-old Subaru wagon was the sportiest car around. She took a space near the exit, thinking that was smart in case she needed to make a quick getaway. She remembered what Ben had said about the building being surveilled. It made her feel safer, knowing that some cops, somewhere, were watching her back.

Or, if you looked at it another way, they were watching her go into a place known for drug traffickers and junkies.

Charlie stared up at the sad, squat building. Twelve units total; six on the bottom, six on top. Cinder-block walls painted a dull gray, a rusty railing lining the second story, rotted-out wooden doors with faded plastic numbers, a low roof with a rotting overhang. Every door had a plate-glass window next to it, and every window had a whining air conditioning unit underneath. A steep pathway led to a filthy-looking pool. Unlit tiki torches circled the chain-link fence. The place reminded her of the airport

34

motels her mother had forced them to stay in every vacation because they were cheap and close to mass transportation. Charlie's clearest memories of Disney World were her night terrors that the wheels of an airplane were going to hit her head while she slept.

"*What do you think we'd get in the lawsuit?*" her father had asked when she had shared with him the reason for her screaming.

Charlie pulled her purse onto her shoulder as she got out of the car. Hot air hit her like a slap to the face. She was sweating by the time she turned around and locked the car door. The smell of fried chicken, pot and cat urine—which was either from a bunch of cats or from a bunch of meth—stung her nostrils.

According to the Girl Scout roll, the Faulkners resided in unit three on the bottom floor, smack in the center, which was probably the worst of all worlds. Neighbors on each side, always waiting for the other shoe to drop upstairs. As she walked across the parking lot, she heard the distinct bass of Petey Pablo's "Freek-A-Leek".

Earring in her tongue and she know what to do with it…

The music got louder as Charlie navigated the broken sidewalk.

With my eyes rolled back and my toes curled…

"Ugh," Charlie groaned, repulsed by the words and also irritated that she knew them by heart. She hated to trot out one of those *in my day* sentences, but she could still remember how reviled Madonna was for singing about her feelings of renewed virginity.

Without warning, the music stopped.

The silence tickled the hairs on the back of Charlie's neck. She had the distinct feeling of being watched as she walked along the uneven path to unit three. The wooden door was warped, painted a dark red that did not hide the black underneath.

She raised her hand. She knocked twice. She waited. She knocked again.

The curtains rustled. The woman's face behind the glass looked older than Charlie, but in a hard way, like the few years had been spent on a construction site or, more likely, in prison. Her eyeliner was a thick black line. Blue eyeshadow. Heavy foundation reminiscent of the coating of Doritos dust on Charlie's steering wheel. She wore her shoulder-length bleached blonde hair in a "Barracuda"-era Nancy-Wilson-style feather.

She saw Charlie and scowled before closing the curtains.

Charlie stood on the hot sidewalk listening to the air conditioning units grumble in the quiet. She looked at her watch. She was wondering if she had been given the brush-off when she heard sounds from behind the door.

A chain slid back. A deadbolt was turned. Then another one. The door opened. Tendrils of cold air caressed Charlie's face. The whining a/c competed with OutKast's "Hey Ya!" playing somewhere in the darkened room. The woman at the door was wearing jeans and a cropped red T-shirt with a Georgia Bulldog on it. A half-empty bottle of beer was in one hand, a cigarette in the other. Her fingernails were filed to long, sharp points, the polish bright red. She reminded Charlie of the trashy Culpepper girls who had relentlessly hounded her throughout high school. The woman had that *look* about her, like when the shit went down, she was ready to scratch out some eyes or pull out some hair or bite down real hard on an arm or a back if that's what it took to win the fight.

Charlie said, "I'm looking for Maude or Leroy Faulkner."

"I'm Maude." Even her voice sounded mean, like a rattlesnake opening a switchblade.

Charlie shook her head. There had to be two different Maudes. "I mean Flora's grandmother."

"That's me."

Charlie's chin almost hit the ground.

"Yeah." She took a hit off her cigarette. "I was seventeen when I had Esme. Esme was fifteen when she had Flora. You can do the math."

Charlie didn't want to do the math, because grandmothers had buns and wore bifocals and watched *Hee Haw*. They didn't sport cropped shirts that showed pierced navels and drink beer in the middle of the day while OutKast played on their boom box.

Maude said, "You gonna keep wasting my air conditioning or you gonna come inside?"

Charlie stepped into the apartment. Cigarette smoke hung like dirty yellow lace in the air. There was no light except for what came in through the slim part in the curtains on the front window. Brown shag carpet cupped the soles of her sneakers. The cluttered kitchenette was part of the living room. The bathroom was at the end of a short hall, a bedroom on either side. Clothes were everywhere, unopened cardboard boxes, a sewing machine on a rickety table shoved against the wall by the kitchen. A large television set was jammed into the corner by the front window. The sound was muted as Jill Abbott screamed at Katherine Chancellor on *The Young and the Restless*.

"Leroy?" the woman said.

Charlie blinked her eyes until they adjusted to the darkness. Across from the TV was a dark-blue couch. A large man overflowed from the matching recliner. A metal brace encapsulated his left leg. He had likely been handsome at some point in his life, but now a long, pink scar ran down the left side of his grizzled face. His lank, brown hair hung to his shoulders. He looked either asleep or passed out. His eyes were closed. His mouth gaped open. His red University of Georgia T-shirt matched the woman's. His jean shorts were not the usual knee-length variety, but cut short enough so that they did not impede the metal brace, which meant they were also short enough to offer up a display to whoever walked through the door.

"Jesus, Leroy." Maude punched his arm. "Tuck your ball back in. We got company."

Anger flashed in Leroy's rheumy eyes, then he saw Charlie and the look was quickly replaced with one of contrition. He mumbled an apology as he turned in his chair and made some discreet adjustments below the waist.

Maude flicked her silver Zippo, lighting a fresh cigarette. "Goddamn idiot."

"Sorry," Leroy apologized to Charlie again.

Charlie did not know whether to smile or run for the door. Peep show aside, there was something off-putting about Flora's grandfather. If he had been handsome in his youth, it was the skeevy kind of handsome where you didn't know if the guy was going to ask you to dance or follow you to the parking lot and try to rape you.

Or both.

"All right, missy." Maude blew smoke toward the ceiling. "What the hell do you want?"

"I'm Charlotte Quinn. I spoke with—"

"Rusty's gal?" Leroy smiled. His bottom lip caved in where his teeth should've been. Given his age, she assumed this meant he'd graduated from pills to meth. "I think the last time I saw you was before your mama died. Come closer so I can get a look at ya."

Charlie stepped closer, though every muscle in her body told her not to. It wasn't just the skeeviness. There was a sickly, chemical smell about him that she recognized from her clients who were detoxing at the detention center. "How do you know my dad?"

"Had me some troubles in my youth. Then I got straightened out, and this happened." He indicated his leg. "Ol' Russ helped me wrangle with the insurance companies. Good man, your father."

Charlie wasn't used to hearing people compliment her father, so she allowed herself a moment of pride.

"Screwed over those bastards for me," Leroy said, and her pride dropped down a few watts. "Tell me whatcha need."

"A beer?" Maude swirled the dregs in her bottle. "Something with a little more bite?"

"No thank you." Charlie spoke the words to the woman's back as Maude opened the fridge door. Dozens of beer bottles tinkled against each other.

Maude selected one, then used the bottom of her shirt to twist off the cap. She tilted back her head and drank down half the contents before she looked at Charlie again. "You gonna just stand there or are you gonna start talking?"

"If Rusty needs some help..." Leroy held up his hands, indicating the apartment. "Not much we can do for him."

"No, it's not that. I'm here on behalf of Flora."

Maude glanced at Leroy. "I told you your little princess was up to no good."

Leroy's easier nature was gone. He sat up in his chair. He leaned toward Charlie. "You one of her teachers?"

"Why the hell would a teacher be here?" Maude demanded. "School's been out for summer since—"

"Teachers work over the summer," Leroy said.

"No, they don't. They barely work during the year."

Charlie jumped in, saying, "I'm a friend." She realized how weird that sounded. Not many fifteen-year-olds had twenty-eight-year-old friends. "A fellow Girl Scout."

Maude said, "I thought that was what's-her-bitch? Melinda?"

"Belinda. She's the leader. I was speaking at the meeting this morning."

"Shit." This came from Leroy. "You're a lawyer, right? 'On behalf of Flora.'"

Maude caught his train of thought. She asked Charlie, "What bullshit did that girl put in your head?"

Leroy jumped back in. "The wrong bullshit, I can tell you that right now."

Charlie wasn't going to let Meemaw and Paw tag-team her. "It doesn't seem like bullshit to me."

Maude snorted a laugh. "She tell you about the trust? You trying to get your dirty little hands on her money?"

Leroy snorted again, too. "Fucking lawyers. Always trying to steal what don't belong to them." He pointed his finger at Charlie. "That stuff I said about your dad—he could go to prison for that shit. Don't think I won't flip on him."

The threat fell short of its mark. Charlie knew her father played it fast and loose with the law, but he would never be so stupid as to get caught, especially by a loser like Leroy Faulkner. She told him, "Your granddaughter wants to file for legal emancipation from you."

Neither Leroy nor Maude spoke for a moment.

Leroy cleared his throat. "Emancipation, like she thinks she's a slave?"

"No, you dumbass," Maude said. "It means she'll be an adult in the eyes of the law. That we won't be her guardians anymore."

Leroy scratched the scar on his cheek. His expression was hard enough to send a chill down Charlie's spine.

He said, "Over my dead body that girl gets emancipated."

Maude said, "She probably wants to live with Nancy. Or Oliver, more like."

Charlie asked, "Oliver?"

"Nancy's brother. They been dating since she was fourteen."

Charlie felt blindsided. Flora had left out the boyfriend.

"He's nineteen years old," Maude said. "Only wants her for one thing."

"That thing won't be worth shit once he's finished with it." Leroy stared at the TV. "Stupid girl."

Charlie felt her mouth go dry. She tried to break down what Leroy had said, to decipher what he meant about Flora's worth. Was he just a run-of-the-mill sexist asshole who thought a girl's value was wrapped up between her legs, or was he a super-predator asshole who didn't want someone else ruining his good thing?

For her part, Maude seemed oblivious to the remark. She told Charlie, "Oliver already has a rap sheet as long as my dick. He ain't got a job, ain't got no prospects for a job. Hell, Flora might as well stay here as soon as live with that dipshit."

Leroy jammed a finger Charlie's way. "You can go back and tell her this ain't gonna happen."

"Damn straight," Maude agreed. "I'm not letting that child run wild. It'll be exactly like with her mother, only worse because she'll blow through that money like it's water."

Charlie asked, "What happened to the Porsche?"

Another prolonged silence followed the question.

"What Porsche?" Maude locked eyes with Charlie, even as she put the beer bottle to her mouth. The end tipped up. Her throat worked like a goose being readied for pâté as she drank down the contents.

Leroy shifted in his chair. Charlie realized he was trying to work up enough momentum to stand. Just as she was reflexively reaching out to help, he hurled himself up to his feet.

He said, "Get some fresh air with me, will ya?"

"Watch yourself," Maude warned her husband, but she didn't try to stop him.

Leroy walked stiffly, swinging his straightened left leg out like he was part of the Queen's guard as he propelled himself toward the door. He let Charlie leave first, then followed her with the same awkward gait.

Charlie squinted in the unrelenting sunlight. Tears rimmed her eyes. She had left her sunglasses in her car.

Leroy said, "Thiss'a way."

She followed him down the broken sidewalk to the side of the building that backed onto a forest. This was the kind of thing that Ben had warned her about—being led out to a secluded location by a man that set off so many warning signs in her head that Charlie might as well be living inside the siren at a fire station.

Still, she followed him. Leroy's leg was busted up. She could easily outrun him, or overpower him, or kick him in his bad knee.

Unless he had a gun.

"Here." He was breathless when they finally reached the covered area by the pool. There were two rotting picnic tables, each with two coffee cans filled with cigarette butts.

Instead of sitting down, he leaned on the edge of one of the tables. He kneaded his left hip with his fist, hissing out a slow sigh of pain. The pink scar on his cheek was more pronounced in the bright sunlight. The wound must have taken a zillion sutures. The right side of his face had nearly been cut in two.

He said, "Flora's a good girl, but she gets things in her head sometimes and you can't stop her from doing them."

"It doesn't seem like she did this on a whim." Charlie didn't know how much to say. She had no proof that Leroy was molesting his granddaughter, but a junkie was a junkie, and she had learned the hard way that you couldn't trust someone who had lost their free will to addiction.

Leroy said, "Her mama, Esme, was the same way. Just headstrong. It's what got her killed. At least, if you ask me. The day she died, Esme got into a fight with her mama, then she grabs Flora, jumps into the car, skids out onto the highway and the next thing we know, we're getting a call from the hospital."

"Flora was in the car with her mother?"

"Eight years old." Leroy stroked the scar like a talisman. "Ambulance man said they found her cradling Esme's head in her lap, just bawling, 'cause half the thing was hanging off. Her head, I mean. Semi-trailer whacked her sideways, nearly took off her head. Does things to you, watching your mother die like that." He looked embarrassed. "Well, I guess you're probably the only other gal in town who knows exactly what that feels like."

Charlie slowly nodded. After several tries, the man had finally hit the mark.

"Well." Leroy fished into the front pocket of his shorts

for a pack of cigarettes. "I guess you figured out real quick that I'm not the best role model."

Charlie let her silence be her answer.

"I'm going to rehab first thing in the morning." He caught her look. "Yeah, I bet you heard that before, but I ain't never said it before. Hand to heart. I'm sick of it, is all. Not doing it for Flora, though God knows I love her. Not doing it for Maude, or because it's the right thing to do. I'm just plain damn sick and tired of feeling like shit all of the time."

Charlie guessed this was a better reason than most addicts could cite. Then again, he was an addict, so he could be lying. If Charlie were in his shoes, if her meal-ticket granddaughter was about to be taken away, she would probably do exactly what Leroy was doing—give the old song and dance about changing her evil ways.

Leroy picked up on her thoughts. "Yeah, you think it's bullshit, right?"

"I do."

Leroy shook out a cigarette, then flicked his lighter.

Charlie watched him suck down half the cigarette before he huffed a plume of smoke into the otherwise fresh air.

He said, "You can ask your daddy about me. I was an okay guy until this." He tapped the side of his brace. "Not the best guy, but an okay guy. Paid my bills on time. Took care of my family. Made sure there was food on the table, a roof over their heads. A good roof, not like this shithole here."

Leroy took another drag as he stared up at the depressing apartment building.

He said, "Hot as a damn scorpion's ass in there when the sun's hitting noon. I just sit in there and bake and watch my programs and I'm thinking—What kind of life is this? What kind of example am I setting?"

Charlie studied the lines in his old face. She was usually pretty good at reading people, but she couldn't get a bead on Leroy Faulkner. Even his face was duplicitous. The side with the scar showed what he said he used to be: an okay guy. The side without the scar showed a junkie who looked willing to do anything to get his next fix.

Leroy said, "When you lose your mobility, you start to think, well, what's the point? And it took me a few years, but I'm seeing the point is that I gotta get up every morning, shave and shower, put on some clothes, and stand up like a man." He tapped the metal brace again. "So what, I need help standing? Not many people can make it on their own these days, ya know? You see them boys coming back from the Middle East, got one leg gone, two legs, an arm, blown up in the head so they can't talk right or think right or even piss straight on their own. Who am I to wallow on my ass like some kind of baby 'cause I fell off a ladder?"

Charlie still couldn't decide whether or not he was laying out the truth or stringing her along. But really, neither scenario mattered because she was here for Flora, and Flora had made it clear what she wanted.

She told Leroy, "I hope rehab works out for you. I really do. But Flora can't wait to see how this turns out. She's still a kid, and there's only so much time she's got left before she's an adult."

"I know that." He looked up at the building again. "She's at that age where there's a fork in the road, you know what I mean? She's either gonna end up like you or end up like Maude. Or, hell, end up in jail, she don't watch what she's doing. Especially with that Oliver fella.

45

Kid's just as crooked as that father of his—if he swallowed a nail he'd end up shitting out a corkscrew."

Charlie decided to take advantage of Leroy's expansive mood. "I could go back to my office right now and draw up the paperwork relinquishing your parental rights."

"Not gonna happen, baby doll." Leroy stubbed out his cigarette in the coffee can. "She's my grandchild, my own blood. I'm not gonna let anybody take her away from me."

"Surely you can see she'd be better off not living here."

"I would be, too. So would Maude. What the hell does that have to do with anything?"

"Flora's only got two years left before she's legally an adult anyway. If you let her go now, that fork in the road is going to turn into a straight line to college."

He laughed. "You Quinns always know how to turn a phrase."

"Are you hurting her?"

Leroy's head snapped around. "Is that what she said?"

"You didn't answer the question."

"And I ain't never gonna."

Charlie tried to give him a way out. "You need to let her go, Leroy. You don't want me asking you these questions in a courtroom, under oath, in front of a judge."

He looked at her, maybe for the first time. Or maybe leered at her was a better description. His gaze traced down the V-neck of her shirt, then rested squarely on her breasts. He caressed the scar on his face with the tips of his fingers. He licked his lips. "You're a good lookin' woman. You know that?"

Charlie fought the urge to cross her arms. She had a sudden, nervous, shaky feeling, like she was trapped.

Leroy sensed her unease. This was the creepy guy at the

46

bar who didn't know how to take "no" for an answer. This was his true nature. He leaned in closer, openly looking down her shirt. "I like a gal got a little fight in her."

Charlie felt her jaw clench. If he was trying to intimidate her, he had picked the exact wrong words. Her fear evaporated, replaced by anger—at herself for almost letting him get to her, at him for being such a bastard. She wasn't trapped. She was a grown woman with a degree from one of the top ten law schools in the country.

She leaned in closer, too, her face inches from his. "Hey, asshole, a fight is exactly what you're going to get. I'm helping Flora with this case. I'm going to do everything I can to make sure she gets away from you."

Leroy was the first to break eye contact. He looked back at the building. Maude had come out of the apartment. She was standing on the stoop, watching them.

He said, "Whatever you got planned for me, that's me. You're gonna have to pry that girl from Maude's cold, dead hands, 'cause she ain't never letting her go."

Charlie recognized the sleight of hand. "Do you really think a judge is going to buy that your wife didn't know what was going on in the next room?"

"You're going down a bad road there, missy. You can fuck with me all you want, but you try to take on Maude—" He shook his head. "You remember this moment when I warned you."

"You remember this moment when I call you to the stand and the bailiff tells you to put your hand on the Bible and swear that you never touched your granddaughter."

He kept his gaze on his wife. "You got proof of what you're saying? You gonna ask Flora that same question after she swears on the Bible?"

47

Charlie couldn't tell if his certainty came from knowing that he was innocent of the crime or if it came from knowing that Flora would protect him at all costs.

There was only one more card that she could play.

She asked, "What if I go to the police and tell them you're a junkie and your wife's been embezzling money from Flora's trust fund?"

Leroy gave a sharp laugh. "I'd tell you to go to the graveyard and ask your mama what happens when your daddy's clients feel threatened."

3

Charlie took the long way back to her office, which added an extra but much-needed five minutes to her trip. The moment she'd left Leroy Faulkner at the picnic tables, her hands had started shaking. The morning queasiness had returned. She'd been forced to pull over to the side of the road and hang her head out the door as she waited for the Doritos to make their return. Only luck and force of will had kept them down.

Charlie had been threatened by clients before. It came with the job when you were defending criminals. Most of the threats thus far had been of the idle variety, usually from a client who felt desperate about his possible prison term. Many more had been of the stupid variety, usually from a client who was on a recorded payphone line at the detention center.

This was the first threat that had actually made Charlie scared.

Her mother.

Murdered in front of Charlie's eyes.

A disgruntled client of her father's holding the shotgun.

Charlie shuddered so hard that her teeth rattled in her head.

She could still see Maude standing outside the open door to her apartment, swilling another beer, smoking another cigarette, as her beady eyes followed Charlie to her car. Or at least toward her car. Charlie had forgotten where she had parked, so she had to double back before finding her Subaru at the end of the lot. Sweat had dotted her upper lip as she cranked the engine. A glance in the rear-view mirror as Charlie had pulled onto the road had shown Maude still tracking her progress.

Meemaw made the Culpepper girls look like amateurs.

Thankfully, Charlie's stomach had settled by the time she pulled into the parking lot behind her father's office building. The additional five minutes on her drive had brought her some calm if not clarity. She still needed to talk to Nancy's parents. It was almost three thirty. The Pattersons would probably be home from work around five. Charlie would have to find the strength to go talk to them in person. A phone call would've been easier, but that was the coward's way out. She needed to see the home, assess the parents' willingness and ability to take care of Flora so that she could honestly tell the judge that the girl had a safe place to land.

That Charlie still wanted to help Flora despite the danger was a congenital defect, likely passed down from her father. Over the years, Rusty Quinn had represented defendants from every side of the spectrum, from abortion clinics to the zealots who tried to blow them up, from undocumented workers to the farmers who got caught hiring them under the table. The blowback on the family had been substantial. When Charlie was thirteen, their house had been firebombed. Eight days later, both her mother and sister had been shot by clients of Rusty's who thought they could make their outstanding legal bills go away.

Charlie should have taken a lesson from her father's losses, but if anything, they had made her want to fight harder.

As Rusty often said—

You're not doing your job right if nobody's screaming at you.

Charlie parked in her usual space behind the office she shared with her father. She got out of her car. Every single step she took toward the building, she found a visual reminder of how dangerous her father's detractors could be: the rolling security gate that required a six-digit code to open, the twelve-feet high fence with razor wire, the multiple CCTV cameras, the thick bars on the windows, the security gate on the steel back door, the lighted alarm panel beside it.

Charlie punched in the code. She used her key to engage the giant bar lock that bolted the door into either side of the steel jamb.

The first thing she smelled was the odor of her father's unfiltered Camels. Then the weird dampness that permeated the carpets. Then cinnamon buns.

Charlie followed the delicious smell to the office kitchen. Lenore was standing in front of the refrigerator. She was almost thirty years older than Charlie, but she was dressed in a pink miniskirt and matching heels. Her eyes were on the television set mounted on the wall. *The Young and the Restless.* This time, Katherine Chancellor was screaming at Jill Abbott. Charlie was only mildly ashamed that she knew the characters on sight.

Lenore said, "You look like hell, baby."

"I'm off my feed," Charlie said, even as she eyed the

cinnamon buns on the table. "Do you know Maude and Leroy Faulkner?"

"I wish I didn't." Lenore put her hand to Charlie's forehead. "You don't have a fever. Were you sick?"

Charlie did not answer, but Lenore's frown indicated she had figured it out.

Lenore said, "Stay away from the Faulkners. He's an oily turd and that bitch will cut you with a knife."

"Good to know." Charlie sat down at the table. She picked at the edge of the cling wrap on the cinnamon buns. Lenore always made them with apple sauce and almond milk in deference to Charlie's lactose issue.

She told Lenore, "Maude's granddaughter wants to be emancipated from her grandparents."

"She gonna pay you?"

Charlie laughed.

Lenore took over on the cling wrap, expertly removing the film without messing up any of the frosting. She found a plate in the strainer by the sink. "What about Dexter Black?"

"What about him?" The man's name had taken on a Voldemort quality. "You're not going to tell me anything that I don't already know."

"When has that ever stopped me?" Lenore opened a drawer. She found a spatula and slid a cinnamon bun onto Charlie's plate. "I saw on your call log that you had a message from Visa."

"Crap." Charlie had forgotten about the phone message at home. She dug around in her purse and pulled out the statement. She should call them back, but she suddenly felt too tired to do anything. She stared at the pages, yawning so hard that her jaw popped.

Lenore asked, "Baby, are you okay?"

"I'm—shit." Charlie saw the problem with Visa now. The minimum amount owed was $121.32. According to Charlie's own handwriting, she had made the check out for $121.31. She was going to get hit with a late fee because of a freaking penny. She scanned the statement until she found the grace period. She was one day off. "If I had seen this yesterday, I could've paid them without being penalized."

Lenore studied the bill over her shoulder. "Not last week, baby. Two weeks ago. Today is the eighth."

"No it's not."

Lenore pointed to the wall calendar.

Charlie stared at the date until her eyes blurred. "Shit."

"This will make you feel better." Lenore pushed the plate toward Charlie as she sat down. "You want to know about Leroy Faulkner?"

Charlie had to force her gaze away from the wall calendar. "What?"

"Leroy Faulkner, Maude's husband. He's one of Rusty's repeats, started using him back in the eighties."

Charlie folded the Visa statement in two, pulling a Scarlett O'Hara so she could think about it tomorrow.

Or maybe the day after.

Or next week.

Lenore continued, oblivious. "Leroy was into mostly petty crimes, boosting weed eaters and mowers from week-enders' cabins, but then he went over the line with a John Deere golf cart, which graduated him from misdemeanor theft to a felony."

Charlie silently played back Lenore's words in her mind so that she could understand what she had been told. In the end, she was not surprised by the escalation. Most people did not wind up in prison because they were smart. She asked, "What happened to his leg?"

"He was working maintenance at the blue jean factory before it moved to Mexico. Climbed one of those old wooden ladders to change out a light bulb, but the ladder broke. Leroy fell straight down, feet first. One of his legs was longer than the other, so it took the full weight of the fall. Crushed the bones up to his hip."

"How tall was the ladder?"

"Thirty feet."

"Good Lord."

"Yeah, it wasn't pretty. I saw the X-rays from the hospital. His foot was folded up behind his calf like a clam shell."

Charlie thought about the brace on Leroy's leg. Was he too disabled to chase after his granddaughter? Flora was young, but she looked like she could handle herself. All she had to do was briskly walk away. Then again, if she was being assaulted by her grandfather, a man who had taken over as her father when her own father had died, then she might not feel like she could run away from anything.

"About his injury." Charlie looked up at Lenore. "I was wondering if—"

Lenore held up a finger to stop her. The woman's hearing was bat-level precise. Three more seconds passed before Charlie heard the humming and snapping and clicking that announced her father walking up the hallway.

"What warm delights!" He clutched his chest at the sight of them. "Two beautiful women in my kitchen. And cinnamon buns!" Rusty helped himself to a pastry. "Tell me, ladies, what does a thesaurus eat for breakfast?"

"A synonym bun," Charlie answered. "I was asking Lenny about Leroy and Maude Faulkner."

Rusty raised an eyebrow as he took a messy bite of

bun. He had no qualms about talking with his mouth full. "Last time I dealt with those two, Maude had sliced open Leroy's face with a switchblade."

Charlie felt a chunk of broken glass pump through her heart. "Any particular reason?"

"The magic of inebriation, I assume. Leroy refused to press charges once he sobered up." Rusty took the paper napkin Lenore shoved in his face. "It's a love/hate relationship. They love to hate each other."

Charlie asked, "Do you think they'd ever turn on each other?"

"Absolutely, but then they'd turn right back." Rusty grinned around another bite of pastry. "Those two are the proverbial finger and the asshole. You can never tell who's fucking who."

Charlie had long become anesthetized to her father's colorful remarks. She did not want to, but she looked at the calendar again. She could feel a sheen of sweat on the back of her neck. She worked to stay with the problem at hand, asking Rusty, "What do you know about their granddaughter?"

"She lost her mother in a terrible accident."

"Are they capable of taking care of her? I mean, like, without hurting her?"

He gave her a curious look. "What are you asking?"

Charlie did not know how to ask her father if Leroy Faulkner was a pedophile. Even if Rusty knew, he was likely bound by attorney–client privilege and couldn't tell her. "Do you think she's safe with her grandparents?"

"People make bad decisions when they're down on their luck."

"So, she's not safe?"

"I did not say that." Rusty grabbed up another cinnamon

bun. "I will, however, tell you that back when the girl's mama died, the fact that there was a trust fund went a long way toward convincing them that they should raise her. Like tying a pork chop around a kid's neck so the dog will play with her."

Charlie wasn't surprised by the news. "What happens when the money runs out?"

"Indeed."

Another non-answer. Charlie tried to narrow down his options: "They only pretend to love her because of the money in the trust? Or do they really love her, even without the money?" She groaned. "How much money did you get for Leroy after the accident?"

"Forced arbitration," Rusty answered, which meant that the case had not been handled by a judge and jury, but by a professional arbitrator who likely worked for the company that was being sued. "Most of the money went to the doctors and the hospital and rehab. Not much left after that. His greedy lawyer sucked up all the rest."

Charlie looked away as pieces of pastry fell from his mouth.

Rusty took another bite. "Anything else, Charlie Bear?"

Charlie held up her hand. "You've been so helpful already."

He was immune to sarcasm. "You are most welcome, my beloved daughter."

Rusty left, snapping his fingers, humming until the cinnamon bun got caught in his throat, then hacking a cough that sounded like the late stages of tuberculosis.

Charlie asked Lenore, "Why do you put up with him?"

"I don't, really." Lenore told Charlie something Rusty would not: "Your dad cut his fee in half to help out, but

Leroy walked away with around fifty grand, which is a lot, but not a hell of a lot."

"Is Leroy on disability?"

"I doubt it. He wouldn't be able to qualify because he's a convicted felon. Can't get food stamps or housing or any government aid."

"I don't guess Maude has a job?"

"She's got plenty of beer money," Lenore said. "And she's at Shady Ray's more than your father, so she's pulling an income somehow."

"Do you know her?"

"Just around." She winked at Charlie. "I'm at Shady Ray's more than your father, too."

"Is Maude making the beer money on her back?"

"I guess there's a certain type of man who'd pay to screw her, but I can't think there's enough kink in this pissant town to keep her gainfully employed."

Charlie could not disagree. Neither could she see Maude Faulkner prostituting herself out. Running a bevy of prostitutes, maybe, but not doing any of the dirty work herself.

Which meant that the woman's beer money had probably been siphoned from Flora's college fund.

Lenore asked, "You okay, baby?"

Unbidden, Charlie's eyes had gone to the calendar again. "They threatened me. Leroy did, but Maude was clearly on board."

"Is that why you look so pale?"

Charlie made herself look down at the half-empty pan of cinnamon buns. Her mouth watered at the prospect of the sweet, warm goodness, but her arms felt too tired to move.

"Charlotte?"

Slowly, reluctantly, Charlie's gaze returned to the

calendar. She stared at the numbers, willing them to roll back. This wasn't only about the Visa bill. She had lost an entire week. How had that happened?

Lenore asked, "How was Belinda this morning?"

"Angry," Charlie said, because there was no better description. "She was angry the first time she was pregnant, too."

"She's not angry because she's pregnant. She's angry because her husband's a dick."

"She said that men change when you have children."

"Ryan was always a dick. It's what made him a good soldier." Lenore held her hand. "What is it, honey?"

"What was Mama like when she was pregnant?"

Lenore smiled. "Excited. A little scared. Radiant. I never believed that bullshit about pregnant women glowing. I mean, what are they, light bulbs? But with your mama, it was true. She glowed with joy."

Charlie smiled back. She had thought the same thing about Belinda this morning.

Lenore continued, "You sister was a happy accident, but with you, everything was planned. She told your daddy exactly when it was going to happen, what you were going to be named, what subjects you were going to love in school, what you were going to be when you grew up."

"Was she right?"

"Don't be ridiculous. Your mother was always right about everything." Lenore added, "And she loved you and your sister to her very last breath."

Charlie had witnessed her mother's last breath. She knew that Lenore's words were true.

Lenore said, "Not all men are assholes."

"I know." Charlie picked at the cinnamon bun until a piece flaked off.

"Ben is a wonderful human being."

"I know that, too."

"So." Lenore sat back in her chair. She studied Charlie. "Are we going to talk about how your period is a week late?"

Charlie crammed the cinnamon bun into her mouth so that she didn't have to answer.

4

Jo and Mark Patterson lived in a newly developed section of town where trailer parks and chicken farms had been replaced by massive five- and six-bedroom houses on three-acre estate lots. This was the sprawliest of urban sprawl, people who were rich enough to live in Atlanta, but successful enough to make the two-hour drive to the city once or twice a month to check in on their investments before heading back to cleaner, easier living in the country. Ben and Charlie often made caustic jokes about the hideous McMansions, but the truth was that they were jealous of the bonus rooms and four-car garages and especially the swimming pools.

The Pattersons only had a three-car garage, which made her feel weirdly sorry for them. From the street, the brick and stucco semi-Tudor style looked crisp and clean, but as Charlie pulled down the long drive, she saw that some of the paint was peeling back from the trim. All of the garage doors were closed. An older-looking BMW was parked in the driveway. Charlie had hoped she'd be early enough to accidentally run into Oliver, Flora Faulkner's alleged boyfriend, but she gathered from the MY KID IS AN HONOR STUDENT AT PIKEVILLE HIGH SCHOOL bumper sticker that Jo Patterson was a stay-at-home mom.

Charlie checked back through her notebook, because she had already forgotten the Patterson girl's name.

Nancy.

Charlie found her Dorito-dusted pen. She had put on her list that she needed to talk to Flora's teachers at school, but she should go ahead and check out Nancy Patterson, too. And she might as well throw Oliver Patterson into the mix. He was likely long-gone from school, but teachers tended to remember bad kids, and Charlie guessed by the fact that Oliver already had a criminal record that he had been memorable in high school.

There was a low rumble of a car engine gurgling from the street as she got out of her Subaru. Charlie watched a stunning, sapphire blue Porsche Boxter roll past the driveway. If she had to guess, she would say the scrawny young man behind the wheel was approximately nineteen years old with a rap sheet as long as Maude Faulkner's dick. The boy who could only be Oliver Patterson had a shock of bright yellow hair and a flattened nose that had clearly been broken many times over. Oliver saw Charlie and pushed his wrap-around sunglasses up on his head. He narrowed his eyes at her, his lips pursed. He was trying to be a badass, but all she could think was that he looked like a capuchin monkey.

The tires screeched as he hooked a sharp U-turn around the cul-de-sac and sped back the way he had come.

"Okay," Charlie mumbled, wondering what that show was about. If Oliver Patterson was really Flora's boyfriend, then the girl needed a lesson about the frying pan and the fire.

She hefted her purse onto her shoulder and turned back toward the house. Up close, the peeling paint gave way to rotted wood and large patches of missing stucco. Some of the bricks were chipped. There were large cracks in the walk as she approached the front door. Weeds sprung up between the gaps. The lawn was patchy, like a dog with mange. The leaves on the boxwoods in front of the porch were curling from some kind of fungus. One of the panes in the bay window was broken; others were fogged up between the double layers of glass. Some shingles had fallen from the roof and landed in the yard. The porch steps were rotted. Even the paint on the front door had faded from red to almost pink.

Charlie had dealt with her share of rich people. Either the Pattersons were from old money and they didn't know how to take care of things or they were from new money that had run out too quickly.

She remembered what Leroy had said about Oliver being as crooked as his father. Charlie cursed herself for not looking into the family before coming over. Her intrinsic nosiness, her joy of delving into other people's business, was paramount to her job as a criminal defense lawyer. Normally, she knew more about her clients and potential witnesses than they knew about themselves. Not this time. She didn't even know how Mark Patterson made a living. Or didn't, if that turned out to be the case. She was too distracted today, taking too much of what she was being told at face value.

The doorbell was Scotch-taped over, so she knocked four times and waited. Then she knocked again, but harder, thinking a more timid sound would go unheard in the gigantic house.

Charlie watched another car roll by. The neighbor across

the street, she assumed, as a brand-new Mercedes pulled into the driveway opposite. A woman got out with her suit jacket over one arm and a briefcase hooked on the other, personifying the clip art of a working mother. She stared openly at Charlie, her nose wrinkled as if she could smell out Charlie's purpose for being on her neighbor's front porch.

"Hello?"

Charlie jumped back, almost falling down the steps. The front door was open. A petite, forty-ish woman in black yoga pants and a neon green tank top stood with a water bottle in one hand and a shotgun in the other.

"Shit!" Charlie's hands went up, though the barrel of the gun was pointed down.

"Oh, sorry. It's not loaded. At least, I think it's not loaded." The woman set the shotgun down beside the door. She wiped her forehead with a towel. She had that slight glisten of rich-people sweat that came from doing Pilates or yoga or some other form of stretchy exercise that took a lot of time and money to learn.

She told Charlie, "I thought you were our neighbor from across the street. I was upstairs working out and saw her car. She's such a bitch. Knocks on the door every day giving us shit about this or that—like it's any of her business." She motioned for Charlie to come in. "You must be the lawyer?" She didn't wait for an answer. "I'm Jo Patterson. Flora told us you'd be coming over. Such a wonderful young woman. Did you know she sold the most cookies of anyone in the state? Plus, she's Nancy's best friend. Those two are like peas in a pod. We just love her to bits. Do you want some iced tea?"

Charlie felt like she needed to shake her head to make the jumble of information settle into a sensible, linear pattern. "No, thank you."

"Let's go to the back. Only a matter of time before that bitch knocks on the door."

Charlie was delighted to follow her to the back, mostly because she'd always wanted to see inside one of these big houses. Jo pulled closed huge, wood-paneled pocket doors as she walked down the hall, mumbling apologies about the mess. In her wildest dreams, Charlie couldn't imagine having so many rooms, let alone how to decorate them all. Jo Patterson had apparently run into the same problem. There was a den with nothing but two beanbags and an old tube TV with a gaming console underneath. The dining room was absent a table and chairs. The chandelier was listing sideways as if someone had tried to swing from it. Even the powder room showed signs of neglect. The wallpaper had rolled down from the ceiling. Someone had made a half-hearted attempt to tear it off, but that had only made it look worse.

Charlie asked, "How long have you been here?"

"Five, six years?" She shut another door to what had to be an office. There was a metal desk like they gave high school teachers, metal filing cabinets with heavy locks, and boxes and boxes overflowing with papers. "We're remodeling, but I've been saying that for a while now because I simply cannot make a decision. There are too many choices, you know what I mean?"

Charlie would love to make the decisions if it meant a new dishwasher that didn't flood if you put more than four plates on the bottom rack.

Jo said, "Here we go." She held out her arms, indicating a large family room and kitchen. Sunlight streamed in from the humongous windows. The vaulted ceiling was at least thirty feet overhead, wooden beams making it somehow feel homey. The back of the house, at least, had been decorated. It was the only part that looked lived in. Deep leather couches. Recliners. A giant flat-panel TV mounted above a stone fireplace. There was an open concept kitchen that made Charlie's eyes water with jealousy—not because she was a cook, but because she wanted a kitchen that made people's eyes water with jealousy.

If they didn't want to adopt Flora, Charlie would gladly offer herself up as a replacement.

"We're not lawn people," Jo said, as if Charlie had asked a question about the muddy back yard. "It's a thing with the neighborhood, because there's some kind of bullshit line in the covenants for the home owners' association about yards and we were, like, 'So what?' but apparently you can't take a crap around this place without getting permission. But, hey, you're a lawyer, right? Could you help us get them off our backs? All they are is a bunch of whiny bitches with nothing better to do."

Charlie had to shake her head again to make sense of the request. "I'm not a real estate lawyer, but I can give you the name of one."

"Nah." She waved her hand, indicating Charlie should follow her into the kitchen. "They'll just charge us for it."

Charlie didn't point out that she would've charged them, too.

"Sweet or unsweet?"

Charlie hadn't asked for tea, but she wanted a reason to stay in the kitchen so she could ogle the stainless steel appliances. "Unsweet."

"Flora is amazing. We couldn't love her more if we tried." Jo jerked opened the glass door of the Sub-Zero fridge. The glass rattled. She had to muscle the door closed. She told Charlie, "Nancy met Flora on the first day of school, and they got along like a house on fire. Always have. Two peas in a pod." She found two clean glasses in the Miele dishwasher beside the scratched apron-front sink. "I was really worried when Mark moved us up here from Roswell, but it's all worked out. He's a real estate developer. That's where he's at now, scouting out some new property for some developers up from Atlanta who want to build an Applebee's off of the North 40. Applebee's! Can you imagine? What's next? An Olive Garden? A Red Lobster? This place'll be hoppin'!"

Charlie sat down at the bar-top counter. The smooth granite was cold under her palms. An empty wine fridge purred beside her. Her jealousy dialed back a notch. On closer inspection, the kitchen looked too lived in. There were scuff marks on the walls. A chunk of wood was missing from the vent hood. Two of the red knobs on the range were missing.

Jo, oblivious to the silent criticisms, poured the tea. "And then there's some other folks looking to build a shopping center off that old mill property on 515. You know the one I'm talking about?" She didn't need encouragement to keep going. "I could totally see a day spa there. I love it up here, but my Lord, it's been hard on my nails, and I think half the people up here would be in a hell of a lot better mood if they could get a decent massage. But look at me talking about myself. What do you need from me?"

Charlie listened to the unaccustomed silence.

"About Flora?" Jo prompted. "What do you need me to say?"

Charlie took a moment to put her lawyer hat back on. "Flora is seeking emancipation."

"Right, she told us that. Remember that Drew Barrymore movie where she was a kid and did the same thing?"

"It's a bit different from—"

"*Irreconcilable Differences*!" She snapped her fingers. "God, that would've driven me crazy, trying to remember the name of that movie. I wonder what happened to Shelley Long? She was so good in *Cheers*."

Charlie couldn't get sidetracked. "With emancipation, what happens is, we all have to persuade the judge that Flora is capable of being an adult—looking out for herself, being responsible, staying off the government's dime. I think we'd be much more likely to win if we could prove that she had a good home to go to."

"Can't get any better than this." Jo spread out her arms with pride, as if her house was not falling apart around her. "But we wouldn't be adopting her, right? She would be living here. Almost like a tenant. But not, like, we have her sign a lease or anything. One of our kids, but not really our kid."

"Exactly," Charlie said, because Flora was still a kid and there was no way she could navigate the world completely on her own. "So, what I need from you in the immediate is for you and your husband to sign an affidavit stating that you're willing to take Flora into your home until she's eighteen years old."

"Oh, hell yes, but more than that." She pushed a glass of tea across the counter toward Charlie. "We'll take her on until she's married. And then she can live in the basement if she wants. We just love her to bits. I said to her the other day—whatever she needs, we are here to give it to her. Anything."

"Anything," Charlie repeated, because there was something strange, almost practiced, about her tone. "What about Oliver, your son? Is he still living here?"

"Of course. He's still my baby."

"Are you hoping they'll get married?"

"Oh, who knows with these kids?" She laughed. "Oliver is so silly around Flora. He used to keep his hair long down to here—" she put her hand to her shoulder. "And he always had zits from the oil in his hair touching his face, and I'd say, 'Ollie, wash that hair and you won't get zits' and he'd slam the door to his room and say, 'Mom!' But then Flora came along and he gets it cut the same way as Mark's, but don't tell Ollie it's the same as his father's because he'll—" She rolled out her lip in a pout, then gave a laugh deep from her belly. Then she kept laughing. And laughing. And eventually, she was laughing so much that Charlie wondered if there was something really funny about this situation that she was missing.

For instance, why was the house falling apart?

Why was the only room that was decorated the only room you'd have visitors in?

Why couldn't they hire a landscaper to do the yard?

Why couldn't they hire a handyman to take care of the house?

And, most importantly, why was Oliver driving a Porsche that, according to Belinda, Maude Faulkner had been driving the month before?

Charlie leaned back in her chair. There was an open door leading off the kitchen, presumably to the basement, which was fine, but the drywall had not been painted, which meant that the basement was unfinished.

"Oh, my." Jo wiped pretend tears from her eyes. "I hope they get married. We all just love that little Flora to bits."

Charlie crossed her arms. "Tell me more about Oliver."

"He's such a gentle, sensitive old soul." She put her hand to her chest, seemingly unaware that she was contradicting herself. "Even when he was a little boy, he was

68

always looking for ways to help people. That's what he wants to do. All of us, really. We want to help Flora, but Oliver feels it more keenly." She leaned against the counter, hand still to her heart. "One time, when Ollie was a little boy, I remember him asking me, 'Mama, why do homeless people smell so bad?' and I was, like, 'Honey, it's because they don't have a home with a shower and a place to wash their clothes,' and the next thing I know, he's talking to this homeless man on the street—in downtown Atlanta—and offering to bring him to our house so he can have a shower and wash his clothes. Of course I couldn't let that happen, but still, it tells you what a sweet heart he has."

Charlie wondered at the woman's practiced tone of voice. She was getting the distinct feeling that she had a front-row seat to the best show in town.

The woman said, "And Nancy is our pride and joy. Sharp as a tack. Not really book smart, but she can figure things out so fast. We're so proud of our little angels. There's my big boy!"

Charlie turned around, expecting to see the family dog, but she found instead an older man with salt-and-pepper hair, a chin cleft that could slice open a bagel, and bronzed skin that had likely been cured under a tanning bed lamp.

"Mark Patterson." He held out his hand, flashing a too-white set of teeth, a heavy gold Rolex and a pelt of hair on the back of his arm that fell in line with having a capuchin monkey for a son. He said, "You must be the lawyer. Flora told us to look for you. What can we do to help?"

Charlie shook his hand, which was damp with sweat. "Tell me what Flora's living situation would be like if she moved in."

His eyes cut to his wife. "Well, she'd be like one of our own children. We'd do everything we can for her. I realize that the emancipation means that she'll legally be an adult, but she's still a sixteen—"

"Fifteen," Jo mumbled.

"Sure, fifteen now, but she'll be sixteen when she moves in. Still a girl, is what I mean. A teenager." He added, "A good teenager. I mean, Flora's stellar, but still a teenager."

Charlie took out her notepad. "Would she have her own room?"

"Of course. We've got plenty of space here."

Jo added, "She might want to be with Nancy, though. Two peas in a pod."

Charlie wished she'd thought to turn the "two peas in a pod" thing into a drinking game, because she'd be drunk by now. She asked, "Could I see where Flora would be living?"

Mark and Jo exchanged another look.

Jo said, "It's a mess upstairs, but I'd be glad to show you another day. Or take some pictures and send them to you. Would pictures work?"

Charlie wondered how many empty rooms she'd find upstairs. And then she wondered how she was going to get the truth out of this couple. "How about a car?"

"A car?" Jo echoed.

"Like you said, Flora will be sixteen soon. She'll need a car to drive."

Again, Jo's eyes shifted her husband's way. The obvious answer would be to say that the trust would pay for Flora's transportation needs, but Mark jumped in with another option.

He said, "Nancy will have a car as soon as she turns sixteen next month. Beat-up Honda I plan to buy off an old client. I imagine they'll share. They always go every-where together anyway. They're two peas in a pod."

The peas/pod thing was like a mantra to this family. In fact, it had almost a rehearsed quality.

Charlie asked, "What about food? Clothing? School fees?"

"Not an issue," Mark said. "Flora is already like a daughter to us. We'll gladly provide for her. She's an amazing girl. We couldn't love her more if we tried."

Charlie saw Jo wince at the statement, which employed the exact same words the woman had used before.

It's like they were going off a script.

Charlie asked Mark, "They get along like a house on fire, do they?"

"Exactly." He beamed, as if he'd passed a test. "Like a house on fire."

"Anyway," Jo said, trying to do clean-up. "The Faulkners, her grandparents, are not good people. I'm sorry to say that, but we are talking about Flora's future here, her college education, her life as a young woman. They try, but their character is—" She stopped herself, probably about to repeat the same line Flora had given Charlie in the bathroom at the Y this morning.

Instead, Jo said, "I know Flora won't say a word against her Meemaw and Paw, but Leroy has a drug problem and Maude is … well, you've met Maude. You know what she's like. I wouldn't cross her for all the tea in China, but we love Flora so much. She's an amazing girl. We couldn't—"

"Love her more if you tried?" Charlie asked.

"N-no," Jo stammered.

Mark jumped back in. "I imagine what my wife was going to say is, we couldn't live with ourselves if we let Flora stay in that awful situation."

"What's so awful about it?"

Mark's well-tanned nose wrinkled in distaste. "That apartment complex is horrible. It's directly off the highway."

"I think that's all they can afford. There's no crime in being poor, is there?" Charlie watched their expressions, which were as fixed as a marble statue. "Unless you mean the trust?"

"Trust?" Mark said, his voice going up at the end. "Why wouldn't we trust her?"

Charlie almost laughed at the poor attempt. "Flora told me that she told you guys about the trust."

The lie made them both relax a tiny bit.

Jo laughed uncomfortably, which was the second laugh in her arsenal, right behind the belly brawl.

Mark said, "Well, we weren't thinking of the trust because, obviously, that's for Flora's college, and to help her get started in life. She's a very smart girl. She could go to any school, really." He indicated the house. "I don't want to sound crass, but, obviously, we don't need the money."

"Obviously," Charlie said.

Jo laughed again, but only twice—a "ha ha" that literally sounded like she was reading it off the back of a box of cereal.

"One more thing—" Charlie always loved the *one more thing*, because it was usually *the* thing. "I'm sorry to say this, but Leroy had some unkind words to say about you, Mark. Something about your being crooked?"

"Oh, dear." Jo gave laugh number one, deep from the belly. "We're standing in the middle of a joke here: a builder and a lawyer walk into a bar…"

Mark joined in, actually clutching his stomach.

Charlie stared at them both until their guffaws gurgled down the drain.

"Ah." Mark wiped bogus laugh tears from his eyes. "Well, you know how people feel about builders. They paint us all with the same brush."

"I thought you were a developer?"

"Builder, developer. Same difference." ·

"Really? One seems much more speculative than the other," Charlie said. "And financially risky."

Jo said, "We do all right. Mark is really good at his job."

"That's great." Charlie waited, looking at Mark as if she expected him to add more.

His mouth was so dry that his lips caught on his teeth when he smiled. "Is there anything else?"

"Nope. Thank you." Charlie closed her notebook. She capped her pen. She pretended not to notice them both exhale in unison. "I'll just need you to put what you said in the affidavit, that you won't ever take any money from the trust."

They did the look again, their eyes bouncing in their heads.

"A letter, you mean?" Jo's voice had gone up, too.

"No." Charlie drank a sip of tea, but only to make them wait. "I'll need a sworn affidavit from both of you saying that you'll never receive any money, directly or indirectly, from Flora's trust." Charlie smiled. "And of course you'll need to take the stand in court and say the same thing, which shouldn't be a problem, right?"

Mark sucked on his bottom lip. "Mm-hm."

She tightened the screw. "Because that would be perjury, if you said that you weren't going to take any money from the trust, but then you did."

"Perjury," Mark repeated.

"Well." Jo cleared her throat. "I'm not a lawyer, but as

73

I understand it, Flora will be emancipated." She smiled weakly at Charlie. "She'll control the money, not us. She can do with it whatever she likes."

"Correct, but if you received money, like if she was a tenant, or she paid utilities or helped with the mortgage or groceries or anything like that, then that would be taking money from the trust. Which is why I'm glad you said she wouldn't be a tenant, because then it might be construed as an inducement to you, as if the only reason you're taking Flora in is to exploit the money in her trust, and since she is still a juvenile and not yet emancipated, the judge would frown on that kind of arrangement. Which is why we need to make it clear that what you said is the truth: Flora would be like one of your own children. Not a cash cow to bail you out of whatever financial straits you might find yourself in." Charlie put her notebook in her purse. "Right?"

Mark did another, "Mm-hm."

Charlie said, "The thing is, the judge would assign a social worker and a trustee to follow up on everything, because taking a child away from her blood relatives, emancipating her as an adult, all with the understanding that she would be looked after by a kind and loving family, is a really big deal. He'd want to make sure that everyone was doing what they'd promised to do. The social worker would make spot checks. The trustee would oversee the outgoing money to make sure everything is above board. And of course everyone would be concerned with the perjury thing, because that can carry a prison sentence of five years and a fine of up to two hundred and fifty thousand dollars."

"Good-good-good," Mark said. "Good. To. Know."

"It is," Jo chimed in, her lips quivering around a smile.

"And I have no problem signing that. Our intention is to not touch a dime in that trust."

Mark caught on quickly. "Jo's right. We have every intention of making sure Flora has that money for college."

They should've known better than to try to bullshit a lawyer. "I'm afraid intentions aren't the same as legally binding agreements. The judge isn't looking for intentions. He'll be looking for sworn testimony."

Jo said, "Well—"

"Obviously, this isn't about the money," Mark interrupted. "Flora is very important to us. We couldn't love her more." His eyes moved like the carriage on a typewriter. "As you said. Before, I mean. That's what you said. We couldn't love her more if we tried."

Charlie matched his fake grin. "Obviously."

5

Charlie sat in her parked car outside the near-empty diner, which was mostly chrome and red vinyl in a homage to the fifties. A quick call to the courthouse that she should've made this morning had revealed that Mark Patterson was millions of dollars in debt. The Range Rover she had seen parked in the driveway when she left the house was about to be repo'd. The balloon payment on the McMansion was in arrears. He even owed some swank private school down in Roswell so much money that they had turned him over to a collection agency.

Obviously, they wanted Flora for her money. Whether they had worked out an agreement for cash up front or monthly rent or something else untoward was a question that Charlie needed to get answered before she proceeded with any of this.

There were other questions, too.

Flora had said she wanted to get away from her grandparents before they depleted all of the money in her trust. Why go to the trouble of emancipation only to fall into the clutches of two different adults who wanted her money just as badly? Did Flora think she could keep the Pattersons on a tighter leash once she was legally declared an adult?

There was only one way to find out, and that was to ask Flora herself, but Charlie had found herself seized by inertia once she had pulled her car into an empty space in front of the diner.

Why hadn't Flora been honest with Charlie in the first place? Was she afraid to tell the truth, or was she playing Charlie for a fool?

Through the windows, she watched Flora talking to her last customer. She looked the same as she had this morning: like a perfectly nice, girl-next-door kind of teenager. Earnest. Honest. A bit fragile, but at the same time, also a bit determined.

The girl's hair was up in a bun. She was wearing a white apron over her blue jeans and the green Girl Scout shirt. Flora's customer was a lean, beef-jerky-ish old man with a comb-over, the kind of guy who had a lot of boring stories for pretty young girls. Flora seemed game to listen. She smiled and nodded, then nodded and smiled, then carefully slipped the bill onto the table before walking away.

Comb-Over slapped her on the ass.

Charlie gasped.

Flora had obviously handled this before. She grinned, wagging her finger at the dirty old man, before returning to work. He practically drooled as she leaned over to clear plates from a recently vacated booth.

Charlie's cell phone rang. She recognized Ben's office number. He had probably found out from the surveillance crew that she had been at the apartments.

She waited for the phone to stop ringing, guilt niggling at her conscience.

77

When she looked back at the diner, Flora was laughing, her mouth open, eyes closed. There was a second waitress, a girl about Flora's age, who had likely said something funny. That seemed to be the long and short of the other girl's contribution to the job. She had made a huge mess of filling up the catsup bottles. There was so much red on her apron that she looked like she'd come straight from a serial murder. Her bleached-blonde hair and the snake tattoo on her forearm weren't doing her any favors, either.

Charlie shook her head at the snake. Used to be, only bikers and outlaws had tattoos. They were so commonplace now that they weren't even a statement. Unless the statement was, "Look, I'm like everybody else."

Her stomach clenched. She was doing it again, acting like an old lady. Or maybe not an old lady. Maybe she was acting like a *mother*.

She put her hand to her stomach and thought of Scarlett O'Hara watching Rhett walk away.

There was a lot to be said for letting tomorrow be just another day.

She shook these thoughts from her head, returning her attention to the scene inside the diner.

Comb-Over heaved himself up from the table. Flora gave him the same perky grin right up until he turned his back to leave. The disgusted look on her face was one that was familiar to a lot of women whose wages depended on whether or not they could convincingly flirt with a man for whom they felt absolutely no attraction.

Charlie couldn't sit in her car for the rest of the day bemoaning the plight of women in the world. She turned off the car engine and headed for the diner.

A rush of cold air enveloped her body as Charlie pushed open the glass door. She smelled French fries, which made her hungry, then she saw a jar of mayonnaise, which brought back the queasiness. Charlie focused instead on the gleaming chrome trimming every surface. There were worse places you could eat. The red vinyl booths were deep and welcoming. The Beach Boys were playing through the speakers. The only other customer in the restaurant was a large man at the lunch counter who was showing an ample amount of butt crack. Charlie guessed by the way he was dressed that the plumber's van in the parking lot was his.

The tattooed young waitress looked up from pouring a cup of coffee and smiled at Charlie. Her name tag said NANCY. She nodded toward an empty table in the front. "I'll be right with you."

Charlie scanned the restaurant, but Flora was not there. "I'm going to use the restroom first."

She walked down the back hall, the same direction in which Flora had disappeared. There were three doors on the left, each marked with their respective purpose. GUYS. DOLLS. STORAGE. The back door was propped open. Sunlight cut across the black-and-white tile floor like a razor. Charlie smelled cigarette smoke. She heard laughter.

"No, you asshole," Flora said, her voice sounding a lot older than before. "I'm not gonna do that. Gross."

"Why?" a man's voice responded. It was high-pitched, likely from a capuchin monkey. "Don't you love me?"

"If *you* loved *me*, you wouldn't even bring it up."

Charlie closed her eyes. At fifteen, she'd had similar conversations with boys.

"Look," Flora said. "Just be cool for a few more days. That lawyer lady is going to talk to your folks, and then we'll both be living in the same house and it'll be easier."

"Not if your Meemaw has anything to do with it."

"I can handle Meemaw."

He barked a short laugh. "If you say so."

"Of course I say so." Flora paused. "Come on, baby, don't be that way."

Charlie listened to the unmistakable sound of lips and tongues coming together.

Which was creepy, because eavesdropping on Flora making out with her boyfriend was something that Comb-Over would do.

Charlie backed up and went into the DOLLS room.

The smell of bleach stung her nose. One of the waitresses, probably Flora, had done a good job cleaning the place. The sink practically sparkled. Even the floor was squeaky clean.

Charlie blinked as her eyes started to blur. She felt unaccountably dizzy. Her stomach was churning again. She pressed her hand to the wall. She was not going to throw up the cinnamon bun from an hour ago. But just in case, she walked into the stall. The toilet seat was already up from being cleaned. Charlie stood there, looking at her reflection in the flat surface of the water, and waited.

Was she going to throw up?

She was going to throw up.

She leaned down. Her stomach clenched. Her throat did that goose pâté gurgling thing, but nothing happened.

She waited a few seconds to make sure. She stood back up. She went to the sink.

The mirror showed a panicked-looking woman on the cusp of her entire life changing.

For the better? For the worse?

Her hand went to her stomach again, not because she felt sick but because she wondered what was in there.

She could go to the drugstore. She could buy one of

those tests. She could pee on a stick and in minutes she would have her answer.

Did she really want to know?

Charlie pulled her hair into a ponytail and clipped it in place. She found some lipstick in her purse. She was smoothing color onto her pale lips when the door opened.

Flora asked, "You okay, Miss Quinn?"

"You keep finding me at bad times." Charlie talked to the girl's reflection in the mirror. "Was that Oliver, your boyfriend?"

Flora leaned back against the wall. She talked to the mirror, too. "I wouldn't say he's my boyfriend."

"Whatever he is, don't do anything with him that you don't want to do."

"I won't."

She seemed very sure of herself. Charlie asked, "Did your grandparents tell you that I spoke with them?"

"Meemaw called. She's really mad at you."

"She made that clear when I saw her." Charlie couldn't pretend that things had not changed since the last time Flora had caught her puking in a public restroom. She told the girl, "I spoke with the Pattersons, too."

Flora leaned back against the wall. She crossed her arms. She waited.

"You know that they want money from you, right?"

Flora looked down at the ground.

Charlie put the lipstick back in her purse. "I can't help you if you're not honest with me."

"I *was* honest," Flora insisted. "I need to get away from Meemaw and Paw. They're going to burn through my trust and—"

"Do you have some sort of arrangement with the Pattersons?"

Flora did not respond.

"I need to know the truth, Flora."

The girl gave in with a slow nod.

"Honey, the Pattersons are not good people. They're scamming you."

"You can't be scammed if you know what's happening."

"That's not altogether true." Charlie crossed her arms, too. "What happens in a year from now when they want more money?"

"I won't give it to them."

"And they'll kick you out, and then what?"

"Then I'll live somewhere else."

"Flora—" Charlie didn't want to get into the minutiae, so she kept it simple "As a lawyer, I can't put someone on the stand to testify if I know that they are going to lie."

Flora looked dubious. "How can anybody prove what you know and what you don't know?"

"I'll know." Charlie let out a long sigh at the girl's confused expression. "This might be hard to believe, but lawyers are held to a code of professional responsibility. I could lose my license to practice if I violate the code."

Flora was unmoved. "You some kind of chicken?"

Charlie wasn't going to give a child a child's answer. "I'm sorry, but I think I am."

Her eyes flashed with anger. "Your daddy ain't no chicken."

"No, but he taught me a very hard lesson about how your choices have consequences." Charlie could see that the girl still wasn't getting it. "My father made some decisions as far as how he was going to be a lawyer that had a lot of negative ramifications for his family." She didn't know how to be any clearer. "Our house was burned down."

Flora looked surprised. She had grown up in Pikeville, so she obviously knew about the shooting. The fact that the house had been firebombed just over a week prior tended to get overshadowed by the cold-blooded murder.

Charlie said, "Someone threw a Molotov cocktail through the front window of our house."

"What's a Molotov cocktail?"

"In our case, it was a glass bottle of gasoline with a rag hanging out of it."

Flora looked confused. "It just exploded when it hit the house?"

"No, they lit the rag on fire before they threw the bottle through the front window. The bottle broke, the gas spread everywhere, the burning rag ignited the gasoline and by the time the fire department showed up, the house was nothing but a smoldering black pit."

"Holy crap." Flora did not look as horrified as Charlie had expected. "Like in *Endless Love*."

"No, nothing like *Endless Love*. More like endless hell." She had forgotten what it was like to be Flora's age. Everything was either tragic or romantic. Charlie said, "Fortunately, we weren't home. The fire spread so fast that the house was gone in less than ten minutes."

Flora pressed together her lips. "I'm real sorry that happened to you, Miss Quinn. That sounds hard."

Not as hard as what had happened eight days later. "Flora, I feel for you, and I want to help you, but the decisions I make as a lawyer, how I defend my clients, what lines I'm willing or not willing to cross, can have far-reaching ramifications. My family depends on me. Especially now." Charlie looked down. Without thinking, she had pressed her palm flat to her stomach. "There's more going on with me than you know about."

"I'm sorry, Miss Quinn. Is there anything I can do?"

Charlie's heart broke at the girl's persistent eagerness to help. "Thank you, but you and I are not out of options. I'm not going to make any promises, but if you're willing to speak up, I'm certain I can work with a judge to appoint a new executor to your trust. Your Meemaw and Paw are gaming the system, and we can put a stop to that. It won't return the money that's been lost, but it will stop the bleeding."

"You'd have to tell the judge why, though." Flora had immediately spotted the problem with the strategy. "I can't do that, Miss Quinn. I'd have to expose them to the law, and then they'd go to prison, and then I'd be put in a home. I'd be better off paying Mark and Jo."

Charlie wasn't so sure the Pattersons would welcome Flora without her money. "That doesn't seem like a good option."

Flora said, "If I don't live with them, then where do I go? To a home?" She shook her head vehemently. "There's some kids at school in foster care. They show up with their heads knocked sideways, lice in their hair, half starved, and sometimes worse. I'd be better off staying at home, losing all my money, than having to sleep with a knife under my pillow every night. If I even get a pillow."

Charlie could not argue the point. Being lost in the Pikeville foster system was tantamount to being lost in a black hole. Things could be especially bad for teenagers like Flora. There were already hundreds of older kids warehoused in substandard living conditions all over the county because no one else was willing or able to take them in.

Still, she told Flora, "We can take this one step at a time. I can talk to—"

Flora said nothing, but two tears rolled down her cheeks.

"It's not a lost cause," Charlie tried, but if she wasn't willing to go after her grandparents for fraud, there weren't many remaining options. "It's only two more years. Maybe I could talk to them, and explain—"

"No." The tears were coming in earnest now. "It's okay, Miss Quinn. I put up with it this long. I can take it for a couple'a more years."

Charlie felt like she had swallowed a rock. As usual, there was something she was missing. She was used to being lied to; helping criminals was not its own reward. But Charlie had lived with the distinct feeling all day that there was an important detail, or perhaps many details, that Flora was holding back.

She asked the girl point-blank. "What do you mean? You can take what for two more years?"

Flora wiped her eyes. "It doesn't matter."

"Flora." Charlie stood in front of her. She gripped the girl's narrow shoulders. "Tell me what's going on."

"It's nothing." She shook her head so hard that her tears flew from her eyes.

"Flora—"

She sniffed. She kept her gaze on the floor. "Do you remember with your mama, the way you'd have a really bad day, or something awful would happen, or you would just be really sad, and you'd put your head in her lap and she'd stroke your hair and everything, no matter how bad it was, just got better?"

Charlie could not swallow past the lump in her throat.

"You just kind of feel it in your body, every muscle letting go, because you know that when you got your head in her lap, you're safe." Flora wiped her nose with the back of her hand. "Aint' nobody can do that for you except your mama, you know?"

Charlie could only nod.

"I miss that so much sometimes. More than her smell. More than her singing. Just that feeling of being safe."

"I know." Charlie also knew if she followed the girl down that sad, lonely road, she would end up sobbing on the floor.

She stroked back Flora's hair. "Baby, tell me what's really going on between you and your grandparents."

"I'm okay."

"You're clearly not okay." Charlie smoothed back another strand of hair. Flora's skin felt hot. Her face was red and splotchy. "Tell me what's going on." She waited, but Flora said nothing. Charlie asked the same question she had asked this morning, the same question that had troubled her from that moment on. "Is Paw hurting you, Flora?"

Her throat worked. She looked away.

"Flora, I can help you, but—"

"It's Meemaw." Flora blinked, trying to clear her eyes. "It's nothing I can't take."

Charlie was momentarily too stunned to speak. Never in a million years had she suspected Maude of abusing her granddaughter.

She finally asked Flora, "What's she doing to you?"

Flora's throat worked again. She was clearly reluctant, but she eventually gave in. She untucked her shirt and rolled up the hem. She pulled down the waist of her jeans. There was a black bruise on her hip, roughly the shape of a small fist.

Charlie wanted to put her hand over the bruise and somehow magically absorb the pain into her own body. Instead, she asked, "Maude did this to you?"

86

Flora rolled up the short sleeve of her shirt. There were oval bruises on her bicep where someone had dug in their fingers.

"Oh, Flora," Charlie breathed.

"I just want to get away." Her voice was small, quiet in the tiny room. "I don't want anybody mad at me. All I want is to be safe."

Charlie thought about all the things that she should say—that as an officer of the court, she had an obligation to report the abuse, that they would go to the police station this minute and file a restraining order, that she would move heaven and earth to get Flora out of that shitty, cinder-block apartment—but every single solution had one horrible, underlying problem: where would Flora go?

Not to the Pattersons. They would probably slam the door in her face.

Not into the system. Someone as gentle and naïve as Flora would likely disappear into the miasma of neglect—or worse.

Especially if the other kids found out about her trust fund.

"Flora—"

The door opened. Nancy poked her head into the bathroom.

Flora straightened quickly, putting a smile on her face, pretending like everything was okay, probably the same way she pretended every day of her life when someone asked her about her godawful grandparents. "What's up?"

Nancy told Flora, "Oliver's leaving, if you want to say goodbye."

Flora started to go. Charlie grabbed her arm, then winced at the perceived pain because how many times had

Flora been grabbed by Maude? Thrown around the room? Punched in the stomach?

"It's okay, Miss Quinn," Flora said. "I'll figure a way out of this. You take care of your family."

"No," Charlie tried. "I want to help you. I *can* help you."

Flora nodded, but she did not seem convinced. "Lemme go say goodbye to Ollie."

"Then come back," Charlie said. "Come right back and we'll talk this out, okay?"

Flora hesitated, but she nodded again before leaving.

Charlie swallowed, trying to clear the lump in her throat. The bruise on Flora's hip was awful, a kind of sucker punch that Charlie felt on her own body. Who would do that to someone as kind and sweet as Flora? Who could physically abuse a child?

Especially another woman. A mother. A grandmother.

It made Charlie feel sick.

She was going to help this kid. She was going to find a way to do right by her, because that's what adults were supposed to do. People like Flora Faulkner were why Charlie had moved back to Pikeville instead of using her very expensive law degree to make a zillion dollars at a white-shoe firm in Atlanta or New York. She wanted to help normal, everyday people who found themselves in bad places and didn't have anyone else qualified enough or smart enough or someone who just plain damn cared enough to get them out of trouble.

Charlie pushed open the bathroom door, a determined set to her mouth, a smile picking at the corners, because she was doing the one thing that her mother had always told her to do: be useful.

Charlie flattened her palm to her belly again. She had

in her mind the image of Scarlett O'Hara being flushed down the toilet.

Tomorrow was not just another day.

Tomorrow, everything would be different, because tonight, within the next few hours, Charlie was going to go to the drugstore and buy a test that would change everything for the rest of her life.

She was seized by the urgent need to talk to her husband. Charlie never kept things from Ben, at least not important things. And this was an important thing, the kind of moment that they would both remember for the rest of their lives. She would have to do it right. Everything would have to be perfect.

Charlie sat down at the counter. She went over the plan in more detail: First, she would talk to Flora and figure out what came next. The girl was being abused. Immediate action had to be taken to ensure her safety.

Once Flora was settled, Charlie would swing by the drugstore off I-15 on her way home. She'd buy the test. She'd pee on the stick. She'd see the plus sign, or the smiley face, or whatever it was. She wouldn't ambush Ben in the driveway. She would wait until he had changed into his sweatpants, then sit him down on the couch—no, in the bedroom. She would follow him upstairs when he went to change out of his work clothes. Or she would already be in the bedroom wearing something slinky and sexy, laid out like an Orion slave girl waiting for Captain Kirk, and then she would show him the test.

Charlie closed her eyes for a few seconds, then she cleared the image from her mind, because none of that could happen until she figured out how to help Flora.

There was no way Charlie could let the girl return to an abusive environment. Charlie didn't only have a legal obligation to report Maude Faulkner; she had a moral one. Which meant that Flora would not be sleeping at the cinder-block apartments tonight.

So, where could Flora go?

Charlie and Ben taking her in was not an option. Even if Charlie wanted to, there was a clear line she could not cross as the girl's lawyer. Maybe there was someone at the school who would volunteer to take Flora into their home while the courts worked things out. Maybe Leroy Faulkner really would get his act together. If a teacher or administrator could look after Flora while he was in detox, then when he was sober, when he was out of treatment, Leroy could move away from Maude and take proper care of his granddaughter.

Charlie took a deep, calming breath. That was the solution: don't think long term. Think short term. If someone from the school did not step up, surely the Pattersons could be persuaded, or cajoled, or even threatened if it came to that, to take in Flora without a monetary inducement if it was only for a few months while Leroy got his shit together.

Charlie felt a grin tighten her cheeks. She was always happier when there was a plan to implement. She looked past the kitchen, wondering what was taking Flora so long. She was probably relaying to Oliver the conversation in the bathroom. Maybe Oliver, such as he was, would be some kind of ally in making sure Flora had a place to stay while Leroy was in treatment. If the Pattersons still wanted money, Charlie could find a way to pay them. The dilapidated house wouldn't pass the strict safety rules enforced by the foster care system, but maybe Charlie could get a temporary placement, a guarantee of funds, before a social worker had time to inspect the living situation.

Barring that, she could come up with the money on her own. Surely there was a stone lying around that she hadn't yet gotten blood from.

Charlie took another deep breath. She was inexplicably giddy. Everything was falling into place. She should call Ben now. Not to tell him what was going on inside of her body, but to hear his voice. To let him hear the happiness in her voice. A kind of foreshadowing for what was to come. She looked inside her purse. Her phone was in the car.

Charlie got up from the counter. She had her hand on the door to leave when she saw Dexter Black walking across the parking lot.

"Unbelievable," Charlie muttered, her former giddiness slipping from her grasp. This asshole had been killing her mood all day. How had he tracked her down?

She pushed open the door, ready to confront him, but Dexter kept walking toward the side of the restaurant.

Lest Charlie should think he hadn't noticed her, he gave her a sly wink.

"What the—" Charlie felt her brow wrinkle. She looked at her car, then she looked back at Dexter, then she looked at the plumber's van in the parking lot, then she turned back around and looked at the empty diner.

The plumber with the butt crack was gone from the stool, so why was the van still there? And why were all the van windows tinted black? And why was there a giant CB antenna coming off the back bumper?

"Shit," she mumbled. Maude said that Oliver already had a record. There were very few illegal things that nineteen-year-olds got caught up in that did not involve drugs. Flora's boyfriend was probably the idiot Dexter was hoping to trade for his freedom. Charlie had crafted such a perfect, happy plan and now it was going sideways because of her most annoying client. All Flora needed was to get caught up in the little jerk's bullshit.

Charlie turned back around. She walked briskly across the restaurant, mindful that the cops were probably watching her, too.

"Ma'am?" Nancy was sitting on a stool behind the cash register.

"Can you call for Flora?"

"She ain't got a phone."

"No, go down the hallway and call for her out the back door. But don't go outside."

"Why can't I go outside?"

"Because you don't need to put yourself into the middle of what's going on out there."

"Is Oliver being a jerk?"

"Jesus." Charlie was wasting her time. She walked down the hallway. The door was still propped open. She could hear the distant mumble of voices, likely a transaction going down between Dexter Black and Oliver the skeevy boyfriend.

Flora would be caught right in the middle.

Instead of going outside, Charlie pushed open the bathroom door in an attempt at plausible deniability. She was an officer of the court. She couldn't interfere with a police operation. She could, however, stand in the hallway and try to keep the girl out of trouble.

She called toward the open back door, "Flora?"

Charlie waited, her heart pounding loud enough to hurt. How many girls were in prison because their stupid boyfriends told them to hold onto the drugs because the courts would go lighter on them? How many times had Charlie heard the same damn story from a woman facing the next decade of her life behind bars?

"Flora?" She tried a third time, "Flora? Can you come here for a minute? I need your help."

Charlie waited again. And waited.

She took a step down the hall. Another step.

She heard car tires screeching.

A girl screamed.

Cops yelled, "Get on the ground! Get on the ground!"

Charlie jogged down the hallway, her heart in her throat. She skidded to a stop outside the back door. Cops swarmed like hornets, rifles pointing red lasers, their black SWAT uniforms and Kevlar vests making them look like they were hunting Osama bin Laden.

More screaming. More yelling. More tires screeching.

Dexter Black was slammed over the hood of the police car. Oliver Patterson was thrown against the wall. Yet another person was already pinned to the ground, spread-eagled, legs and arms restrained by four different cops.

One of the cops leaned back on his heels. Charlie saw a flash of Girl Scout green as he clicked the mic on his shoulder, telling his bosses, "We've got the suspect in custody."

"Suspect?" Charlie whispered.

That was no suspect.

That was Flora.

6

Charlie paced the interview room as she waited for Flora to be processed through booking. Back at the diner, as the girl was being manhandled into a squad car, Charlie had screamed at the top of her lungs for Flora to keep her mouth shut, but she was terrified her instruction had fallen on deaf ears. Flora was smart, but she was fifteen, and way too helpful for her own good. She likely would not understand that the nice policeman was trying to trick her into prison time.

The only saving grace was that Charlie had witnessed the SWAT team turning out the girl's pockets. They had found a folded stack of ones from Flora's tips, a pack of gum and her learner's permit. When someone had suggested they search the diner for her purse, Charlie had suggested they get a search warrant. And then she had pretended not to notice the look exchanged between Flora and Nancy when one of the cops had said they would have the warrant before sundown. Charlie was a lawyer. She could not allow herself to be party to the concealment or destruction of evidence.

Not to mention she might be looking at a murder rap if she got hold of Dexter Black. He had called her twice today, once without a police monitor. He could've mentioned that he was going to squeal on some teenagers.

Not teenagers.

One teenager.

Flora.

Oliver Patterson had been released without charge. Dexter was free to do as he pleased until the next time his ass landed in jail. Nancy was never formally questioned. The entire sting had been about capturing Flora Faulkner. Why they launched a SWAT team to handcuff a fifteen-year-old girl was beyond Charlie. She was surprised they hadn't brought the decommissioned bulletproof Humvee the police force had been given last year.

The door opened.

Flora was dressed in an orange prison jumpsuit that was too big for her small frame. Her wrists were uncuffed. She hugged herself with her skinny arms. Her pink-and-white Nike sneakers shuffled across the floor. Her eyes were wide, pupils blown. She was clearly in shock.

Charlie's first inclination was to hold the girl, to let her put her head in Charlie's lap, to stroke back her hair and tell her that everything was going to be all right.

Instead, Charlie guided her to one of the chairs. She helped Flora sit. She put her hand to the girl's back, soothing her, willing her to stay strong. If Charlie's brain had been ping-ponging at the diner, it was so focused now that she practically vibrated with the urgency to make sure Flora got out of this in one piece.

She asked the girl, "Are you okay?"

Flora nodded.

"Did you speak to any of them? Answer any questions?"

Her lip started to tremble. She played with the charm on her necklace, a tiny cross that Charlie had not noticed before.

"Flora, look at me." Charlie had to force the girl to turn her head. "Did you answer any questions or talk to anybody?"

"No, ma'am."

"Did you see a guy in a cheap suit?"

"I think so," Flora said. "I mean, the suit was ugly. I don't know how much they cost."

"That's probably Ken Coin. He's the district attorney. You didn't say anything to him?"

"No, ma'am." Flora's eyes brimmed with tears. "Am I gonna go to jail?"

"Not if I have anything to do with it." Charlie kept a protective arm around the girl's narrow shoulders. Her heart was pounding in her chest. She was so worried for Flora that she might as well be talking to her own child. "Listen, that man in the suit, Ken Coin, he is as sneaky as a snake, so be very careful around him, okay? He'll try to trick you, or he'll lie to you about evidence or he'll tell you that your friends have said bad things about you, but don't believe him. All you need to do is sit there and be quiet and let me do the talking."

Flora's tears started to fall. "I'm scared."

"I know you are, sweetheart." Charlie rubbed her back. Her chest swelled with righteous indignation. She wanted to throw open the door, kick the ass of any man who got in her way, and take Flora to safety. "You're going to be okay. I'm going to represent you."

"What about ramifications?"

"It's different now," Charlie said. "We don't have much time before the police come in. I'm your attorney. I'm

96

making it official. Anything you tell me is confidential. Do you understand?"

Flora nodded, her teeth still clicking.

"Is there anything you need to tell me?"

"I didn't do anything."

"I know, baby, but you need to trust me. There's a reason they picked you up."

Her tears kept falling. Her nose started to run. "I don't understand why I'm here."

Charlie found some tissues in her purse. As she waited for Flora to blow her nose, she noticed the girl's hands were clean. At least the booking sergeant had allowed Flora to wipe off the black ink after being fingerprinted. "Do you have any idea why they might have arrested you?"

"No, ma'am."

"Is Oliver wrapped up in something that maybe he shouldn't be?"

"Not that I know about." She looked over Charlie's shoulder, thinking about it. "I mean, he went hunting during the off season, last spring, but he didn't catch anything, so does that count?"

Charlie shook her head at the girl's guilelessness. "He's not selling drugs or mixed up with some bad people?"

"No, ma'am, not that I've ever seen. He mostly plays video games and smokes cigarettes and drinks beer on the weekends." Flora wiped her eyes. She asked, "What's gonna happen to me now?"

Charlie sat back in her chair. She had to dial down her emotional response, otherwise she would be next to useless when Ken Coin made his entrance. "The district attorney is going to come in here and ask questions, but remember, you don't answer anything, or even make a comment, unless I tell you to, okay? And then be very, very brief. Only answer the question he asked. Don't try to be helpful, or over explain."

"Should I answer anything at all?" the girl asked. "I mean, don't I have the right not to? To remain silent?"

"You do, absolutely, and if that's your choice, then you should follow your conscience. What'll happen is you'll say that you don't want to talk to them, and they'll leave, and you'll be taken back to the cell."

Flora took a shaky breath. "What about your way?"

"As your lawyer, I think it's best to let the district attorney talk, and we'll listen, and maybe we won't give him a lot of answers but his questions will help us figure out how you got mixed up in this mess." Charlie added, "I can't promise anything, but I might be able to talk them into releasing you. But you should know that if I can't talk them into it, then you'll be taken back to the cell anyway."

Flora started to nod. "It sounds like your way gives me a chance, at least."

"I can't make any promises," Charlie hedged, because sometimes Ken Coin was smarter than she wanted to admit. "Now, listen, your Meemaw said that Oliver has a record. I know you said before that he wasn't mixed up in anything. I really need the truth from you now. I'm not going to judge you, or lecture you, or pass judgment. I just don't want to be surprised by Mr. Coin when he comes in."

Flora pressed together her lips. "I'm supposed to open the diner tomorrow morning. Nancy can't do it 'cause she's got summer school." Flora stopped to swallow. "You said I have to have a job to prove to the judge that I can take care of myself. I can't get fired."

Charlie let out a short breath. The girl was still worried

about emancipation when she should have been worried about prison. "Is there anything you're not telling me?"

Flora said, "I'm sorry, Miss Quinn, but I can't tattle on anybody. That's not right."

Charlie studied the girl's open expression. Thirty minutes ago, Charlie had been worried about the Pikeville foster system. Now Flora was looking at a night, possibly more, in the women's detention center. She wouldn't make it a day without being irreparably damaged. The older inmates would set upon her like jackals.

Charlie asked, "Who are you protecting?"

Flora said nothing.

She guessed, "It's not Oliver, is it? You're protecting someone else."

Flora looked away.

"Is it Meemaw?" The Porsche. The beer money. Maude was the clearest beneficiary of Flora's trust. She was also keeping the girl in line with her fists. "Flora, listen to me. Someone is going to sleep in jail tonight. Do you want it to be you, or do you want to tell Mr. Coin what Meemaw has been doing and maybe work it out so that it's just you and your grandpa living in the apartment?"

Flora kept looking down at the table. "I don't want to get anybody—"

"In trouble, I know. But if you're taking the fall for Meemaw, think about where this ends."

"I'm a kid." She shrugged. "I won't get in trouble like she would."

"In trouble for what?" Charlie asked. "Hypothetically?"

Flora glanced over her left shoulder, then her right. She saw the two-way mirror. She looked into Charlie's eyes, and she silently mouthed the word *meth*.

Charlie suppressed a curse. She knew from Ben that the cops were looking for a van that was being used to cook meth in the vicinity of the cinder-block apartments. Maude didn't strike Charlie as a meth freak, but Leroy had all the signs. Were they sending their granddaughter to make the buys, then Leroy took some off the top and Maude sold the rest at Shady Ray's for beer money? And was Maude beating Flora whenever Flora refused to make the buys, because the girl struck Charlie as the type of kid who didn't relish the idea of breaking the law.

Charlie told her, "If you go down for a crime your grandmother committed, I want you to know that you're probably looking at hard time. I don't mean jail. I mean big-girl prison."

Flora's throat worked as she swallowed. "I'm only a kid, though."

"There are a lot of teenagers in adult prison who thought they'd get a light sentence because of their age, and they're going to have gray in their hair by the time they get out."

Flora seemed to waver.

"I want you to think about something," Charlie said. "The way the police arrested you, the SWAT team and all the cops, I'm assuming that was to scare you. And you should be scared, but you don't have to be stupid. They're obviously trying to intimidate you into turning on whoever sold you the drugs in exchange for your freedom. It's why they handcuffed you behind your back instead of in front. It's why they took you down in front of your friends, behind the place where you work."

Flora chewed her lip.

"You can give them the name of the van driver and make all of this go away."

"Miss Quinn, those are bad people. They'll kill me."

Charlie had suspected she'd say as much. "Then you can give them the name of the person who sent you out to buy the drugs in the first place. The person who skimmed some off the top and sold it on."

Flora looked shocked. "I can't do that. Turn on my own blood. She took me in when my mama died. She's all I got, except for Leroy."

Charlie tucked the girl's hair back behind her ear. It broke her heart that she was protecting her own abuser. "Flora, I know that you love your Meemaw, and I know that you want to do the right thing, but you have to ask yourself if your loyalty is worth the next five or ten years of your life." She added, "And for that matter, what does it say if your Meemaw lets you go to prison so that she doesn't have to?"

"She wouldn't do that," Flora defended. "She loves me too much."

"She's beating you."

"She gets mad sometimes, is all." Flora added, "I hit her back sometimes, too."

"Is she afraid of you when you hit back? Afraid like you're afraid of her?"

Flora thought about it. The answer was clear enough on her face. "She doesn't mean it when it happens. She's real sorry after. She cries and gets upset and she stops for a while."

"Only for a while?"

"Like I told you, I put up with it this long. I can put up with it another two years." She sniffed. "It only happens once or twice a month. That's forty-eight more times, tops, before I go to college. And most of them aren't that bad. Maybe three or four really bad ones, that's all I'm looking at and—"

"Flora—"

"You know what it's like to not have a mama." The girl was crying openly now. "You know what it's like to not have nobody who loves you, who cares about you, more than anybody else in the world." Her voice cracked on the last part. "She ain't perfect, but that's what Meemaw is to me. She's more of a mother than anybody else I got. You can't take that away from me. Not again."

Charlie felt tears in her own eyes. How many times had she wanted over the years to just one more time put her head in her mother's lap and listen to her say that everything was going to be okay?

"Please," Flora begged. "I can't lose her. You gotta get us out of this."

"Flora—" Charlie cut off the rest of her response when the door opened.

Ken Coin swaggered into the room; inasmuch as a man built like a miniature praying mantis can swagger. He slapped a thick file folder down on the table. He adjusted his too-loose pants. His dyed black hair was slicked back. His suit was so shiny that the fluorescent light turned the houndstooth pattern into a strobe.

Coin had started out his professional life as a sheriff's deputy, then gotten his degree from a law school that was housed in a strip mall. None of the imbeciles who had voted him into office seemed to mind that he knew as much about the law as Flora probably did, or that he was so cozy with the police force that the Constitutionally mandated independence of the judicial system was a running joke at the courthouse.

"Charlotte." Coin gave her a terse nod. He waited for Roland Hawley, a senior detective on the city's police force, to enter.

Roland was a tall guy. He had to tilt down his head as he passed under the door frame. There wasn't much space left in the room once he closed the door.

Coin sat across from Charlie. He tapped his fingers on the file folder like untold mysteries were soon to be revealed. Roland took the chair across from Flora. His football-sized hands went flat on the table. His knees were probably touching Flora's.

Charlie grabbed the girl's chair and pulled her back half a foot.

Roland smiled. They had played these games before. He took a small micro-tape recorder out of his pocket. "Mind if we keep this aboveboard?"

Charlie grimaced. "Don't you always?"

Roland laughed at the sarcasm. Still he waited for Charlie's nod before he turned on the tape recorder.

Charlie said, "Do you want to tell me why we're here?"

"She didn't tell you?" Roland winked at Flora. "Come on, gal, let's get this story told so I can go home to my wife."

Flora opened her mouth, but Charlie grabbed her hand underneath the table, willing her into silence. She told Coin, "Please tell the detective not to speak directly to my client."

Coin gave a heavy, put-upon sigh. Instead of instructing Roland, he said, "Florabama Lee Faulkner, you're gonna be charged with the manufacturing and distribution of methamphetamine, an illegal substance, in quantities in excess of five hundred grams."

Charlie's chin almost hit the table. The quantity triggered a mandatory twenty-five-year sentence. "Drug trafficking?"

"Yes indeed." The smile on Coin's face was somewhere between delighted and smug.

"She's fifteen years old," Charlie said. "You have to prove that she was knowingly involved in—"

"The sale, delivery or possession," Coin finished. "Yes, Charlotte, I am aware of the law."

Charlie bit back a cutting remark about his dime-store degree. "What evidence do you have?"

"We'll leave that for the courtroom."

"You're taking this to court?" Charlie was aware that her voice was registering too high. She tried to get control of her tone before Coin said something about hysterics. She told him, "Flora didn't have any drugs on her, let alone over a pound meth. I watched them search her."

"She had constructive possession," Coin said. "We found the drugs in the trunk of her car."

"She's still got her learner's permit. She can't legally own a car."

Coin fiddled with his paperwork. "A 2004 Porsche Boxter, sapphire blue. Not much of a trunk, but that's where we found it." He slid the deed across the table. "That car is owned in full by the Florabama Faulkner Trust."

Charlie couldn't believe he was truly this ignorant. Even a mail-in law school covered the basics of trusts. "Her grandparents control the money. She can't access it until she's of legal age."

Coin said, "According to the car salesman's sworn affidavit, Flora picked out all the features on the car. Couldn't decide between the Boxter or the 911."

Roland said, "I would've gone with the 911 myself."

Flora's mouth opened to respond.

"No," Charlie warned. "Let me answer the questions."

Roland asked Flora, "That's how you wanna play it? Let your lawyer do all the talking? I thought you were tougher than that."

104

Flora's mouth opened again.

Charlie stuck out her arm, like she needed to physically block any and all responses. To Coin, she said, "Flora is not a drug kingpin. She's an honor student. She's a Girl Scout, for Chrissakes. She's working for tips at the diner, not running a meth operation."

Roland asked, "Tell her that you can do both, Flora."

Flora looked at Charlie, desperate. "I thought you said they wanted a name."

"We've got a name," Roland said. "Florabama Faulkner."

Charlie shook her head. This had to be one of Ken Coin's legendarily stupid power plays. "You know the word of a car salesman doesn't matter. Flora can't access that money."

"She manipulated her grandpappy into doing it for her." Coin made a weird spider-movement with his hand. "Like a marionette pulling the strings."

"That's crazy, Ken. Even for you."

"You think that's crazy?" He pulled a stack of photographs from the file and started tossing them on the table. "Flora driving the Porsche to work. Flora in the Porsche by the lake. Flora driving through the McDonald's off Fifteen. Clearly, this is her automobile."

Charlie scanned the photos and instantly saw the flaw in Coin's reasoning. "Per the restrictions on her learner's permit, she has an adult with her in every picture. That's Leroy Faulkner, her grandfather, in the passenger's seat."

Coin said, "She forced him to go with her. Look at this." He flung over another photograph. Flora was still behind the wheel, but Leroy was passing something out the window to a shifty-looking thug in sunglasses. Charlie immediately recognized the customer: Dexter Black.

So why had Dexter flipped on Flora instead of Leroy? None of this made sense.

Coin said, "We've got detailed audio and video of the drug buy. This fella here bought twenty grams of meth."

"From Leroy Faulkner, not his granddaughter."

"Flora was directing the deal from behind the steering wheel of the car."

"You have that on audio?"

Coin didn't answer, which meant he was relying on Dexter's testimony, which meant his case was built on popsicle sticks.

Roland asked Flora, "Where's the van, sweetheart?"

Flora bit her bottom lip.

Roland told Charlie, "She's got her boyfriend driving around town, cooking meth out the back of a panel van. It was parked twenty yards down from the school this afternoon. Selling that shit like the ice-cream man."

Charlie asked, "Then why didn't you send the SWAT team for the van? Or did you need all of your men to take down a one hundred-pound teenager?"

"She's tougher than she looks." Roland gave Flora another wink. "Right, honey-pie?"

"You still didn't answer the question," Charlie said. "Why didn't you scoop up the van?"

Coin admitted, "We saw it on the security camera after the fact."

Roland leaned over the table. He told Flora, "Don't think we won't find that van eventually, girl. What do you want to bet it's got your fingerprints all over it?"

"Sounds more like it'll have Oliver's prints." Charlie crossed her arms, letting them know she was over this charade. "What do you want, Ken?"

"We want to lock up this very dangerous criminal,"

Coin said. "The grandparents are veritable prisoners in their own home."

"That's ludicrous." Charlie tried to figure out Coin's angle. He was not talking like a man who wanted to make a deal. "If anybody is pulling the strings here, it's Maude Faulkner."

Flora sucked in some air. Charlie put out a hand to still her.

It was Coin's turn to cross his arms over his chest as he sat back in the chair. "I don't play tricks, Charlotte. You should know me better than that."

The cocksucker played more tricks than a Vegas hooker. "You think Leroy and Maude won't let their grand-daughter go to jail, that they'll just step up and confess to—"

"They won't." Flora's voice cracked in terror. "I know they won't help me." Her tears were running so fast that they pooled into the collar of her jumpsuit. "What am I going to do?"

"Be quiet, baby. Let me handle this." Charlie held onto her trembling hand. She told Coin, "Look, the grandparents have been draining Flora's trust for years."

Flora stiffened beside her.

"I'm sorry," Charlie apologized to Flora. "This is serious. Your grandmother is—"

"Not the executor," Roland said. "The grandfather, Leroy Benjamin Faulkner, is the executor of the trust. He makes all the financial decisions. Or at least, he passes on the decisions that Flora makes in exchange for a little taste of that fine product she's been selling."

Coin said, "To make it clear, she's controlling her grand-father, Leroy Faulkner, a man who was crippled in a horrible accident, who used to be a hard-working man, a good man, because she, Florabama Faulkner, got her own grandfather addicted to methamphetamine, the same meth-amphetamine she's got her boyfriend selling out of a panel van."

"Yes, Ken, thank you, that was already clear." Charlie tried to reason with them; they had obviously made a mistake. "I've been working with Flora on legal emancipation. She's trying to get away."

"From what? The good life?" Coin asked. "You're like that mama who says, 'My sweet baby fell in with a bad crowd.' Listen, sweetheart, this girl here, she's the leader of the bad crowd. She's the one everybody's scared of."

Charlie said nothing. Her head was spinning from their outlandish conspiracy theories.

Roland told Flora, "Why do you want to be emancipated? You own them apartments. You can kick everybody out and have the whole place to yourself."

"The trust owns the apartments," Charlie guessed, but she wondered why on earth Leroy would buy the complex. If he wanted meth, there were easier ways to get it. She told Roland, "You said it yourself: Leroy controls the trust. Flora has no decision-making power."

"You ever meet Leroy?" Roland asked. "He seem like a master financial wizard to you?"

Maude, Charlie thought. Flora's grandmother could be pulling the financial strings. She had been driving the Porsche last month. She was the one who camped out at Shady Ray's every night. She was the one who was beating Flora.

Then again, Oliver was driving the Porsche this afternoon.

And there were all those photographs of Flora driving the car.

And what was up with that panel van?

Coin asked, "Why do you think the court wouldn't let Maude oversee the trust? She was bankrupt six times before her daughter died. Spent a nickel in prison for embezzling money from the Burger King she worked at."

Roland chuckled. "That old bitch ain't worth the toilet paper it'd take to wipe her off your shoe."

Charlie opened her mouth to respond, but then she closed it, because everything they were saying had the *sound* of bullshit, but not the *smell*.

And God knew Charlie had smelled some bullshit in her time.

Roland seemed to sense an opening. He told Charlie, "Little Flora here, she's pretty good at getting exactly what she wants."

Under the table, Charlie felt Flora's grip tighten on her hand. She looked at the girl, saw the glistening tears in her eyes, the tremble of her lips, and wondered exactly who she was dealing with.

Roland kept talking. "Like, what are you doing here, Miss Lady? How'd a hot-shit lawyer like you end up being at the diner in the right place at the right time, and now you're here bulldogging this case for a girl you hardly know. Probably for free. Am I right?"

Charlie did not have an answer for him, but her gut was telling her that something was really wrong here.

"The trust owns a white panel van. Same kind of van that was spotted outside the school selling meth." Roland smiled at Flora. "Only the van was reported stolen this afternoon, ten minutes after the campus resource officer walked across the street to confront the driver. Ain't that a funny coincidence, Miss Flora?"

Flora stared back at him.

He said, "*You* reported the stolen van to the police."

"She did not," Charlie tried, but then Roland slid over a piece of paper. Charlie had seen so many police reports in her time that she could probably make a stack of her own. She skimmed the written details. At 3:15 that afternoon, Florabama Faulkner had reported that a white panel van had been stolen from outside her apartment building earlier that morning.

The same van someone was cooking meth out of. The same van that was owned by the Florabama Faulkner Trust. The same van that was selling meth to kids outside the school.

What did it take to run that kind of operation? To consistently elude the police? Customer Loyalty. Business Planning. Marketing. Financial Literacy. Top Seller.

It was Juliette Gordon Low's dream. Every freaking skill Flora had learned in Girl Scouts had found a real-world application.

Charlie felt the slow, free-falling sensation of her heart dropping in her chest.

She was actually believing part of Roland and Coin's story.

And if part of it was true, what about the other part?

She looked down at the girl. Flora blinked back at her, Bambi-style. The girl had rolled in her shoulders. She was trying to make herself look smaller, more delicate, in need of saving by whatever nitwit she batted her eyes at.

A string of curses filled Charlie's head. She had to get out of here. The room was suddenly too small. She was sweating again.

Roland asked Flora, "Your fancy pro-bono lawyer know about your real estate deals?"

Charlie worked to keep her expression neutral. She

110

couldn't leave. She was still Flora's attorney, and standing up and screaming *What fucking real estate deals?* would probably land her in front of the ethics board. She told Coin, "Any real estate purchases Leroy made on behalf of the trust had to be in keeping with the initial guidelines of the trust."

Roland huffed a laugh. "They all moved outta that pretty house on the lake to live in that hellhole because Leroy Faulkner understands the fluctuations in the commercial real estate market?"

"You think Flora does?" Charlie grasped at straws. "Why would a slum be worth more than a house on the lake? There are twelve apartments, total. They can't be bringing in more than three hundred a month each. You think trading down for an income of less than four thou a month, less maintenance, less whatever mortgage they're carrying—"

"She's got Patterson landlocked," Coin provided. "Mark's got all his money tied up in sixty acres of unde-veloped land, got this supermarket and all these restaurants interested in building, but he's got no highway access without her parcel."

"It's not the apartments," Roland said. "It's the direct access that makes that land valuable."

Charlie worked to keep her mouth from dropping open in surprise. She had grown up in Pikeville, seen the influx of builders from the city, even listened to Jo Patterson wax poetic on Olive Garden and Red Lobster, but it had never occurred to her that the Ponderosa was worth anything.

Coin said, "Leona Helmsley over there talked old Mrs. Piper into selling her the land without going through a broker."

Charlie rolled her eyes, but she could feel the last crumbs of disbelief falling away.

Roland provided, "Hoodwinked the widow out of two million bucks' worth of highway access. Tell her what you paid, Flora-girl."

Flora did not answer, but a smile teased up the corners of her mouth.

Coin told Charlie, "She played on the old lady's heart strings, said she had a moral obligation to keep that kind of land in the Pikeville family, stop those greedy developers from ruining the town."

Roland took back over. "And then Little Miss Girl Scout turned around and parlayed it into blackmail for one of the greedy developers." He asked Flora, "You pay the widow in Thin Mints or Tagalongs?"

Flora tittered at the joke.

Charlie wanted to shake her like a Polaroid.

The smell of bullshit permeated her nostrils.

Roland said, "Flora knew Mrs. Piper from her cookie-selling route. Talked the widow into selling her land for less than half a million bucks."

"Three hundred seventy-five thousand dollars, to be exact." Coin slid over a stack of pages. The deed for the Ponderosa was on top. He asked Flora, "They give out a badge for swindling old ladies?"

Roland suggested, "Something with a kid yanking out an old lady's walker right from under her, for instance?"

Coin said, "You gonna answer or just keep sitting there like the cat got the canary?"

Flora's eyebrow raised. She slowly turned her head toward Charlie, that familiar angelic expression on her face as she waited for her hot-shot idiot lawyer to talk her out of this mess.

"Jesus," was the only word that Charlie could push out of her mouth.

There was a flash of white teeth from Flora before she got her smile under control.

Coin asked, "What's that, Charlotte? You need a moment to talk to Jesus?"

Roland snorted a laugh. "More like she just had a come to Jesus moment with herself."

Charlie felt hot and cold at the same time. She tried to swallow but ended up coughing instead. Her throat had gone dry. There was a weird ringing in her ears.

"Charlotte?" Coin said, feigning concern.

"I need ... I should look ..." Charlie held up a finger, asking for a moment. She pretended to read the closing documents from the Ponderosa. The number kept mumping into her line of vision: three hundred seventy-five thousand dollars, roughly what she and Ben owed in student loans. Invested in a dinky piece of land on a desolate strip of highway that might one day turn into a thoroughfare through which half the county traveled.

Charlie got to the last page. She studied Leroy Faulkner's shaky signature.

She finally made herself accept the facts that Ken and Roland had laid out in front of her: Leroy controlled the money, but he was also an addict. Flora trafficked in the drug to which Leroy was addicted. You didn't need to be a world-class economist to figure out supply and demand. Leroy did whatever Flora demanded so long as she kept him supplied. Which meant that Charlie had spent the majority of her day chasing her own tail on behalf of a budding psychopath.

And still, Charlie had an obligation to defend the little asshole.

She had to clear her throat before she could speak. "According to your own paperwork, the Widow Piper sold the land to the trust, not to Flora Faulkner."

Coin smiled. "That's how you wanna play it?"

"It's not a game, and I'm not playing," Charlie told him, because he knew as well as she did that she couldn't simply get up and walk away from Flora. Now that they were here, she had a professional obligation to at least see the interview through. "You have no proof that my client had anything to do with this transaction or anything else. Flora is a minor. She cannot legally enter into any agreements, real estate or otherwise. Her name is not on any of these documents." She let the papers flutter back together. "Leroy Faulkner signed off on everything. The only other signatures are the notrary, the director of trust relations at the bank, and Mrs. Edna Piper. I don't see Flora's name anywhere."

"Here." Coin jammed his finger on the top of the front page where it read PURCHASER: THE FLORABAMA FAULKNER TRUST.

Charlie met his smug grin with a smirk. "Do I need to explain to you the difference between a financial entity set up through common law jurisdictions and a minor child?"

Coin's expression remained unchanged. "Do I need to explain to you about collusion to commit fraud?"

"I think you mean civil conspiracy, which you would know if you'd gone to a law school that wasn't housed between a massage parlor and a Panda Express."

Coin stood up, fists clenched, and walked out the door.

Charlie knew he was pacing the hall. She had seen him do this before. His fuse burned quick, but the explosions tended to be of the premature variety.

Roland ignored the antics, asking Flora, "Did you see a map or a drawing on Mark's desk? Is that how you figured it out?"

"Nope." Flora knew she had lost Charlie, so there was no point in pretending anymore. "*If* I did what you're saying, which I didn't, I'd tell you that I've got two eyes in my head. Anybody can see that land needs a right-a-way."

Roland had the pleased look of a man who understood that criminals loved to brag about their bad deeds. "How'd you find out who owns the property?"

"It's all at the courthouse. Anybody could look. *If* they wanted to, I mean. Not that I wanted to. But *if*."

"And you recognized the old widow's name?"

"Mrs. Piper?" Flora shrugged. "I could sell her the moon *if* I wanted to."

"And?" Roland gave her a second before prompting, "Keep going, little bit. Tell me how you worked it. I mean, *if* you worked it."

"No," Charlie said, because Flora seemed to think her *if*s were some kind of legal krypton. "Flora, my advice as your lawyer is to shut the hell up."

Flora cut her with a look, her eyes flashing like a snake's.

Charlie suppressed a shudder that could've shaken her out of her chair.

"Charlotte, let's figure this out together." Coin stood in the doorway. He had one hand tucked into the waist band of his shiny slacks. His anger had been chased away by his idiotic belief that she could be persuaded to throw her client under the bus. "You need to talk your client into taking a deal or she's gonna be too dried up for anything by the time she breathes free air again."

Charlie said nothing.

Coin tried another track, talking to Roland instead. "I gotta give it to her: gal's got the nose for property."

Roland nodded. "Too bad she didn't know Mark Patterson's broke. He can't afford to pay her market value for the highway access, and nobody wants the apartments without Mark's land attached to the deal."

Flora could not quell her grin. "Good thing I've got the cash to buy Mark's piece when he goes into foreclosure."

"Flora," Charlie tried, literally the least amount of trying she could do. "You need to stop talking."

"I will, Miss Charlie. But you can see they ain't got nothing on me." Flora crossed her arms. She told Coin, "You heard my lawyer. I've talked about as much as I'm gonna talk."

"Good, because I'm tired of pussy-footin' around your bullshit." Coin leaned over the table. He told Flora. "We've got you dead to rights on the drug trafficking, peanut. Come clean and maybe we can shave some time off your sentence."

"I know my rights," Flora shot back. "You gotta charge me or let me go."

Charlie felt her head swivel around so hard that her neck popped. "What did you say?" Flora started to speak, but Charlie held up a hand to stop her. "You're not in cuffs. Did they fingerprint you?" Flora shook her head. "Did they take your photograph?" Flora shook her head again. "Did they ever say you were under arrest? Read you your rights?"

Roland sighed. He switched off the recorder.

"Flora?" Charlie prompted.

"No. None of that."

Charlie asked her, "Why did you change into jail clothes?"

116

"They told me to because my other ones were dirty from being on the ground."

"But they let you keep your sneakers and your necklace." Charlie gave Ken Coin a furious look. "You fuckwad."

Coin shrugged.

She remembered the first full sentence that had come out of his mouth.

"You're gonna be charged ..."

He hadn't said that he was actually charging Flora. Charlie had been so stunned by the possible prison sentence that she hadn't noticed, but now she understood that the district attorney had played her almost as well as Flora had.

She told Roland, "You were part of this. Don't think I'll forget that."

Roland gave another labored sigh.

"I hate men who sigh instead of telling me to fuck off." Charlie told Flora, "Get up." When Flora didn't stand, Charlie pulled her up. She practically dragged the girl to the door, telling Coin, "This is shitty, even for you."

"She ain't gonna be free for long," Coin said. "Only a matter of time before she screws up."

"Unbelievable," Charlie muttered. She kept pulling Flora down the hallway. She punched the buzzer so the desk sergeant would open the door to the lobby.

"I don't understand," Flora said. "What happened?"

"You were never under arrest. There's no way a judge would've signed off on their flimsy evidence, so they swooped down and gave you a twenty-person escort to the police station. They were hoping you would be scared enough to confess."

"Confess to what?" Flora put on her innocent babe-in-the-woods look. "Miss Quinn, I didn't do anything."

Charlie punched the buzzer again. "Shut your lying mouth."

The door buzzed back before it slowly swung open.

Maude Faulkner was in the waiting room. She jumped up from one of the hard plastic chairs. "What the hell is going on?"

Charlie banged open the exit door. She was done talking to anyone connected to these vile people. It was one thing to be lied to by a client. That happened on a daily, sometimes hourly, basis. Flora Faulkner had not just lied. She had manipulated Charlie. She had played off the memory of Charlie's dead mother—a wound that was still so raw that Charlie felt tears in her eyes whenever she remembered that last day, that last breath her mother had taken. Charlie had been sitting inches away from the shotgun. If she thought about it hard enough, she could still feel the hot splash of blood from the buckshot ripping her mother in two.

And Flora had used that tragedy not as a lever, but as a crude weapon. A cudgel. A baseball bat. A Molotov cocktail thrown straight into Charlie's heart.

She spotted her Subaru at the back of the parking lot. Her hands shook as she searched for her keys. The hot and cold was back, the ringing in her ears. She didn't care about the *why* of it all. She just wanted to extricate herself from this awful situation. She had wasted enough time on their crazy bullshit. She had more important things to worry about, like that her entire life was about to change and she had to go to the drugstore to get the test and then she had to tell her husband and he might not be as excited about the news as she was.

Charlie stopped five feet away from the parking lot.

Her burning desire to leave fizzled at the sight of a

sapphire blue Porsche Boxter parked in one of the hand-icapped slots.

The car had to cost at least fifty grand, roughly half of Charlie's student loans. Black interior. Navy blue top. Sparkling in the overhead parking lot lights. And the overhead lights were on because it was dark outside and instead of being home with Ben, telling him how enor-mously wonderful their life was going to be in nine months, Charlie was outside the police station fighting the urge to strangle a fifteen-year-old monster.

She turned around.

Flora was right behind her.

Maude knew enough to keep her distance.

Charlie said, "Nice car."

"It is, isn't it?" She had the beatific smile of a Chuckie doll. "Am I allowed to open my mouth now?"

"Is there something you want to say?"

"It's privileged, right? Strictly between you and me?"

Charlie crossed her arms. "Sure."

"First," Flora said, "thanks for getting me out of there."

"Good luck keeping it that way, you stupid child." Charlie saw the familiar flash of anger in the girl's eyes. "You heard the man in there. They're coming after you, Flora. You'll be forty before you get out of prison. Your life will be over."

Maude grunted. "Shit, wait 'till you're fifty!"

"This isn't a joke," Charlie said. "Flora is in serious trouble. They found over five hundred grams of meth in the trunk of the Porsche."

Maude pursed her lips. "That's some weight."

Charlie wanted to slap the woman. "The district attorney and the police are not going to drop this case. They're coming after her for trafficking." She jammed her finger into Flora's face. "And you're not smart enough to get yourself out of this mess."

"Good thing I've got a lawyer who can be smart for me."

"Not this lawyer," Charlie countered. "I'm done with you."

"Miss Quinn, you can't abandon me." There was a lilting tone in the girl's voice that had worked like a charm a few hours ago. "I need your help."

"Help with what?" Charlie remembered the way Flora had crossed her arms in the interrogation room. The girl's fingers had laid across the three bruised dots on her bicep almost exactly. "You did that to yourself, didn't you? The bruises on your arm?"

Flora looked down at her bicep. She answered the question by pressing her fingers deep into the bruises. They matched exactly. "I thought you might need a visual aid to push you off the fence. Sometimes the sad I-Lost-My-Mama stories only get half the work done."

Charlie thought about what the girl had said about putting her head in her mother's lap and tasted bile in the back of her mouth. "How'd you get the bruise on your hip?"

Flora said nothing, but Maude provided, "She snagged her hip on one of the tables at the diner. What'd she tell you?"

"She told me you were abusing her."

Maude recoiled. "I ain't never fucked a girl in my life."

Charlie wondered at a woman more concerned with being called a homosexual than a pedophile. "She told me you were beating her. She blamed you for the bruises."

"Florabama Faulkner." Maude stuck her hands on her hips. "Why would you tell her that?"

Flora shrugged. "People fight harder when they think you're helpless."

"I would've fought for you!" Charlie shouted. "If you'd been honest about your problem to begin with, I still would've helped you."

"Not like you did in there," Flora said. "You would'a been trying to cut a deal, not helping me take a walk. You got your code, like you said—you don't wanna suffer the ramifications of being a dirty lawyer like your paw."

Charlie let the dig at her father slide. "Is that why you told me about your mother dying? To manipulate me? You know my mother was murdered. What happened to my sister. They were real people. They meant something to me. And all you saw about that tragedy was a way to use me. Is my life all just a game to you?"

Flora looked down. She snubbed her sneaker on the concrete walk. "I'm sorry, Miss Quinn. I know I should've been honest. I promise I won't—"

"You were playing the Pattersons, too, weren't you? You were stringing Mark along, letting him think you'd sell him the apartments if he let you move into his house?"

"He wasn't going to hold onto his land that long. And I've been working with the bank to get that house. I figured I could charge them rent if it came to that." She shrugged. "You might think I'm a bad person, but I'm not in the business of kicking people out of their homes."

Charlie wasn't interested in land deals or rental agreements. She wanted Flora to say the real reason she'd pulled Charlie into this mess. "Your grandfather said he was going to rehab. He's the executor of the trust. If he sobered up, you couldn't bribe him with meth anymore."

"Son of a bitch," Maude hissed. "Stupid bastard left for the clinic an hour ago."

121

Flora said, "That don't matter, Meemaw. The thing about Paw is, there's always something he wants." She gave Charlie a pointed look. "Everybody has a price. Whether it's meth or cookies or a state approved highway access point, all you gotta do is dangle it in front of 'em and they'll jump as high as you say."

Charlie felt the implied dig. Her price had been exactly zero.

"I tried to do this easy," Flora said. "I was being honest when I said I didn't want to get Meemaw and Paw into trouble. I need the money now. Not in two years. Not while I'm waiting for Paw to fall off the wagon. This town is about to take off. More people are coming up from Atlanta. We'll get liquor sales approved any day now. The economy's on the upswing. Right now is the time to buy."

Charlie said, "You're pretty convincing—except for the part where you turned into a drug dealer."

"Three million dollars," Flora told her. "That's the amount of money that was in the trust after the lawyers got paid. It's down to less than nine hundred grand, last time I checked. Putting it into land is the only investment that makes sense. Land never drops in value."

Charlie said, "Your mother wouldn't have wanted this."

"You didn't know my mama."

"No, but I know what mothers are like," Charlie said. "My mother loved me with her last breath, Flora. Her last breath. You were with your mom when she died, same as I was. I know she was the same way with you. She wanted you to do good things."

"She wanted me to survive," Flora countered. "That's what she told me with her last breath, right before that semi near about took off her head. She was yelling at me, telling me to get out of this shitty place and make some-

122

thing of myself no matter who I had to step over to get there. You can't do that with nine hundred grand."

"You can if you don't drive a fifty-thousand-dollar Porsche."

"It was sixty-eight thousand," Flora countered. "And it was leased, 'cause that's better for the taxes. Driving a flashy car is part of the cost of doing business. You've gotta put on a show for people. Success breeds success."

"You sold meth to kids. You hooked your own grandfather—" Charlie ran out of words. Telling the conniving shit that she was hurting people seemed like a vast waste of time. Flora knew she hurt people. That was part of the fun.

Charlie had her keys in her hand. "Don't ever try to get in touch with me again. Don't even think about asking for my help. Or my father's. I'm finished with you."

"Don't worry about me, Miss Quinn. I'll figure something out."

"I bet you will." Charlie wanted to leave, but she could not let it go. She hadn't felt this angry, this used, in a long time. "I was really worried about you. I spent my whole day trying to figure out how to help."

"You *did* help me. You got me outta that mess in there. And you were right about letting them talk, because they told me a lot with their questions."

"What did they tell you?"

"That they don't really have a case. That if it comes down to it, Paw and Oliver look guiltier than I do, just like I meant it to look. That I can wind things down for a while, wait out Mr. Coin's interest, and start back up again when I'm ready." She shrugged. "Like I said, it doesn't matter to me what I'm selling. People want what they want, and if you're willing to give it to them, there's profit to be made."

"You're unbelievable."

"And you're a good person, Miss Quinn. Don't let anybody tell you otherwise." Flora grinned, showing her teeth. "You're honest and fair. Friendly and helpful. Considerate and—"

"Shut the fuck up." Charlie walked toward her car before she got charged with assaulting a minor.

She'd be damned if she let a teenage meth queen humiliate her with the Girl Scout oath.

7

Charlie sat at the kitchen table with a leftover cinnamon bun and a ginger ale. She did not know which one her stomach needed more. Frankly, it did not matter. She was too exhausted to lift her arms to pick up either of them. She could only sit in her chair staring blankly at the salt and pepper shakers on the table.

Ben had bought them when they moved in together. One was shaped like Pepé Le Pew, the other Penelope Pussycat.

"Get it?" Ben had asked. "Pepé is the pepper."

She let her eyes find the clock on the wall. He was late getting home from work. This was one of his on-call nights. The assistant district attorneys took turns catching after-hours cases. He usually called Charlie to let her know if he was running late. Maybe that was the reason her cell phone had rung outside the diner.

Charlie forced herself to stand up. It was cheaper if she checked her phone messages through the home phone. She found the cordless by the fridge where she'd left it this afternoon. Dorito-dust fingerprints were still on the numbers. She heard her cell phone ring in her purse and in her ear. She pressed in the code for her mailbox.

"*Hey, babe,*" Ben said on the message. "*Did you see that call from Visa? Our card number got jacked this morning. Somebody dropped a buttload of cash at Spenser's. Can you believe that place is still open?*"

Charlie hung up the phone.

The YWCA bathroom. Her purse spilled onto the floor.

Flora must have copied the number on the Visa before she put the card back in the wrong place.

"Jesus." Charlie sank back into the chair.

What the hell had happened to her today?

At the age of thirteen, Charlie had stopped trusting people. You didn't watch your mother die in front of you without turning into a cynic. Florabama Faulkner had somehow managed to sneak past Charlie's bullshit detector. The girl was obviously good at deceiving people. Maude had been fooled. Or at least she had let a lot go unchecked. Then again, Ken Coin had seen through the act.

Which hurt on a lot of levels.

Was Charlie really that gullible? Or was Flora really that good?

Ben's car pulled into the garage. His radio was up so loud that she could hear Bruce Springsteen clearly singing about Philadelphia. Or as clearly as Bruce Springsteen was capable of.

She closed her eyes. She listened to his car door open and close. The kitchen door open and close. She didn't open her eyes until his keys clicked onto the hook beside hers.

"Hey, babe." Ben kissed the top of her head. He sat down at the table across from her. "I heard you were at the station today."

"Did you hear why?"

"The boss has been uncharacteristically silent, but I Scooby-Doo'd it out that it pertains to those apartments."

She nodded, knowing she could not fill in the details. Flora was a budding psychopath, but Charlie couldn't break attorney—client privilege. Even if the girl deserved it.

Ben said, "Coin wasn't happy when he got back from the station, so I am assuming you did a good job." He picked up the cinnamon bun and took a bite. He watched Charlie as he chewed. "I thought you weren't going to those apartments by yourself because they're dangerous?"

"I'm sorry I lied."

"I knew you were lying, but I had to get my objection on the record so I could say I told you so."

"You earned it."

"I told you so." He offered her the rest of the cinnamon bun.

She shook her head.

He asked, "Can you tell me what's wrong? No details, just the big picture?"

"I—" Charlie stopped. Her brain felt too tired to do the acrobatics required to tell him something without telling him everything. "Do you think Belinda and Ryan are happy?"

"Oh, hell no."

"Because of the kids? I mean, the baby and the one on the way?"

Ben wrinkled his forehead. "I don't think so. They kind of had the kids because they thought it would fix their marriage, right?"

"Is that what Ryan said?"

Ben made a funny face. "You didn't hear that from me."

She said, "Can you blame him for being unhappy? Belinda's kind of a bitch sometimes. I love her, but—"

"That's not fair." Ben put down the cinnamon bun. "She's not that different from the way she's always been. Ryan knew what he was getting into. If it wasn't working, then he should've told her and given her a chance to fix it. And the same way with him. You work on problems. You don't tear into each other and try to win."

"It's too late now. They're stuck with each other." She added, "At least, Belinda is. She said everything changes when you have kids. That you're trapped. That your husband treats you differently, looks at you differently."

"Well ..." Ben seemed dubious, though he clearly thought this was a philosophical conversation because he knew Charlie always took her birth-control pills. "I used to think Ryan was this manly man because he went to war and all that, but the thing is, a man doesn't treat his wife that way. Or his kids."

"What do you mean?"

"He's always running her down. You heard it last weekend. His daughter is standing there, and he's yelling at Belinda like she's a moron."

Charlie remembered. Belinda had just sat there, publicly humiliated, while Ryan loomed over her. For all her tough talk, she never seemed to stand up to him. Maybe because he spent so much time wearing her down.

Ben said, "If you've got problems, I get that. Everybody has problems. But you don't talk that way in front of your kid. Especially if it's a girl, because you're saying it's okay for men to talk to women that way, and it's not."

Charlie wanted to throw her arms around his neck and kiss him.

He said, "You know, scratch that. It's the same if you

128

have a boy. He's going to learn from his dad that it's okay for boys to be assholes to women." Ben got up and went to the fridge for a beer. "And another thing, look at how Ryan talks to her when they're in public. Can you imagine what happens when they're home?"

Charlie watched him open the bottle. Ben had never yelled at her. He had raised his voice plenty of times, but he never really yelled at anyone, especially Charlie. Even when they fought, which didn't happen often but happened enough, he didn't try to tear her to shreds. He made his point. He said that she was wrong, or unreasonable, or crazy, and she said he was wrong, unreasonable or crazy, and they kept doing that until they ended up having sex or watching a movie.

Charlie said, "I didn't know you felt so strongly about this."

"Let's just say my dad was a perfect example of how not to treat his wife and kids."

Like Belinda, Ben wanted to do things differently.

Charlie gave her husband a better shot at accomplishing the goal than her friend.

She said, "I had this client today. I can't tell you her name."

Ben listened as he drank his beer.

"She's a teenager, but she played me. Big time. I haven't been fooled like that since my sister convinced me that our neighbor across the street worked for the CIA."

"The CIA? Was there a Russia connection?"

"Focus, babe."

He waited.

"Dealing with this girl, it made me wonder what kind of parent I would be." Charlie thought about the small white box in her purse. She had stuck to the plan. Mostly.

On the way home, she had swung by the drugstore and bought the test. She had peed on the stick in the dirty public restroom. And then she had lost her nerve and shoved the thing back in the box before the little plus or minus could show up.

She told Ben, "This client today, who is probably a straight-up psycho, I believed every word that came out of her mouth. She played me like a fucking fiddle. And it made me wonder, if a stranger can fool me like that, what happens if it's my own kid?"

"Well, probably it'll be worse." Ben sat back down at the table. "Think about how many parents you and I have talked to in our jobs where they say, 'Not my boy.' You could show them video footage of their kid stealing a bike out of the rack, then breaking it down for parts, and they'd say, 'Oh, he must've thought that was his bike,' or 'Somebody must have tricked him into doing that.' Their brains automatically come up with an alternate explanation. They can't accept that their babies can do wrong. Hell, even guys on death row still get visited by their mothers. They won't give up on them. I guess that's how it is. You never give up." Ben smiled. "So, if that's the criteria, that you never give up, then your whole life has basically prepared you for motherhood."

Charlie reached out for his hand. An hour ago, Ken Coin had used the same type of example to tell Charlie that she was stupid, and now her wonderful husband was using it to show her that she would be a terrific parent.

She asked Ben, "What about you? Are you prepared?"

"Me?" He laughed. "I was the biggest nerd at my high school and now I've got a smoking-hot wife."

"That's your character reference for being a father?"

"Babe, if a guy like me can land you, what can't I do?"

Charlie couldn't tease him back. "What if I'm really bad at it?"

"You're not bad at anything." He squeezed her hand. "You're perfect."

"You didn't feel that way Friday."

"Okay, except for Friday when you were being annoying, you're perfect." He squeezed her hand again. "Why are you worrying about what kind of parents we'll be? Because Belinda and Ryan are the worst examples in the world?"

"I guess."

"We've got a lot of other friends who are good parents. Or at least trying to be."

He wasn't wrong. So why had Charlie spent so much time focused on their most miserable friends instead of their happiest ones?

She told Ben, "This is why I need you—to remind me that there are good things in the world."

He reached over and stroked back her hair. "If we ever have kids, I can't promise that I won't make mistakes, but I'll show up for it, which is all anybody can really do. Being there is half the battle."

Charlie wiped her eyes.

"What's going on, babe? You've been off since this morning."

Charlie felt her bottom lip start to tremble. She had avoided saying the words all day, but now was the time to say them. Even if the test was negative, she was sure that they were as ready as they were going to ever be to bring someone else into their family. Ben was her soul mate. He was the love of her life. She wanted to watch him be a good father to their child. She wanted to be the fool who insisted that her baby would never bite another toddler, would never throw a brick through a window, would never traffic meth if it came to that, but please, God, don't let it come to that.

"Babe," Ben said. "You're crying."

Charlie wiped her eyes. She wasn't just crying. She was about to start sobbing. She could count on one hand the number of times she had cried like that in front of her husband, and they generally involved a crushing Duke Blue Devils loss on the basketball court.

"Chuck?" He knelt beside her chair. "Are you okay?"

She wasn't okay. She was bawling. Her eyes burned. Her nose was running.

He asked, "Do you want a tissue?"

"There's a pack in my purse."

He stood up to retrieve her purse by the door.

Charlie's heart flipped.

The small white box.

The plan already out the window.

This wasn't how she had planned to tell him, but this was how it was going to happen. She was going to be crying and he was going to open her purse and see the pregnancy test and then he would look back at her and—

The phone rang.

Charlie nearly leapt from her chair.

Ben handed her the purse as he walked to the phone. "Hello?"

Charlie closed her eyes. She listened to his end of the call.

"When?" Ben asked, then, "How many?" then, "Okay." He ended the call.

Charlie opened her eyes.

Ben had put the receiver down on the counter. He'd kept his hand on it like he needed to hold onto something.

Charlie gathered from his serious expression that he had caught a murder case.

Which meant that now was the worst possible time to tell him her news.

She asked, "Do you need to go?"

"I have to wait for the fire department to secure the structure. They don't have all the details yet." Ben sat back down at the table. He held onto her hand again. "The cinder-block apartments."

Charlie felt her heart stop mid-beat.

"They're only cinder-blocks on the outside. The rest is wood."

"What are you saying?"

"There was a fire," Ben said. "The whole place burned down. Six people are dead."

Charlie put her hand to her mouth. Flora. Maude. Leroy.

Ben said, "A kid named Oliver Reynolds was caught leaving the scene. He was driving the meth van they've been looking for. The cops found a bottle in back matching the same bottle that was thrown through the window."

Charlie felt every muscle in her body tense. "Bottle?"

"Yeah, there was a witness. She was out by the picnic tables smoking when she saw Oliver pull up. She watched him light up a rag on a bottle of gasoline and throw it into one of the first-floor units. That's called a—"

"Molotov cocktail." Charlie had told Flora about the incendiary device less than three hours ago. "What's the name of the witness?"

"Like I said, the details are still coming in. I didn't get a name, but she's the girlfriend, or ex-girlfriend, of the kid who did it. They think it was some kind of lovers' spat. She kept talking about that movie—"

"*Endless Love.*"

133

"Yeah," Ben said, but he didn't ask the obvious follow-up question, which was *How did she know?*

"Jesus." Charlie covered her mouth with her hands. She was too afraid to speak. Flora had to be the witness. Flora had probably told Oliver to throw the bottle through the window. Hell, Flora had probably called the police so that Oliver would be caught red-handed.

And then she had told the cops the same thing that she had said to Charlie about the Quinn house being burned down: it was just like *Endless Love*.

She asked Ben, "Who was in the apartment that the fire bomb was thrown into?"

"The witness's grandparents. They died almost instantly. I don't have their names."

Charlie had their names, but she couldn't tell Ben because she had taken an oath to protect her client.

Her client who was now free to become emancipated.

Whose grandparents had burned alive in their own home.

Whose boyfriend was going to die in prison for arson and murder.

Whose best friend's parents were going to lose their home.

Who had figured out how to neutralize a police investigation.

Who was going to make millions off a future land deal.

Who had reached into Charlie's heart when she talked about that safe feeling you got when you put your head in your mother's lap.

Charlie closed her eyes.

She thought about her mother's gentle touch as she stroked back Charlie's hair. Her soothing voice. Her gentle assurances. Her logical reasoning that no matter how bad things got, they would always, always get better. The sharp, hot slap of blood from when the trigger was pulled on the shotgun.

Charlie opened her eyes.

Good thing she hadn't told Flora that part of the story.

Don't worry about me, Miss Quinn. I'll figure something out.

"Chuck?" Ben was staring at her, concerned. "Does the fire have something to do with what happened to you today?"

Charlie nodded. She was crying again, though not from hope this time, but from despair.

How complicit was she in the deaths of Maude and Leroy Faulkner? Oliver already had a record. He would go to prison for the rest of his life. Flora had not only managed to free herself, she had wrapped up the meth-trafficking case in a pretty bow. Any lawyer worth his salt could persuade a jury that the poor girl was a victim of her meth-dealing grandparents and her arsonist boyfriend.

And Charlie had practically written the girl a guide on how to do it.

"Chuck." Ben pressed his lips to the top of her head. "What's wrong?"

"I'm a terrible person."

"Come on, don't say that."

"I am," Charlie cried. How had she been so blind? "I'm going to make a horrible mother."

"I'm not going to let you talk like that." Ben pulled her hands away from her face. "Look at me, Chuck. I know you can't tell me what happened today, but I'm here. I'm always here. Whatever it is, we'll face it together. You and me. Always."

"Do you promise?"

"Of course I promise." Ben held tight to her hands. "I love you."

"I love you, too." She kissed his hands. She thought about what might be growing inside of her belly. "With my last breath."

Another corny line, but true.

Ben gave her his awkward grin. He wiped the tears from her eyes. "I've got at least an hour before they're ready for me. What do you want for dinner?"

She shook her head. She couldn't think about eating.

"Okay, Chef's choice." He stood up and went to the fridge. "Chicken? Hm ... that chicken looks kind of gamey."

Charlie reached into her purse. She found the white cardboard box.

Ben said, "I could do a roast, but I'm not sure about the veggies. I can make spaghetti. Oh, there's still some General Ho's. Do you want—"

"Ben?"

He glanced back over his shoulder. "Yeah?"

"I'm pregnant."